No Other Choice

No Other Choice

A Pride and Prejudice Novella

LEENIE BROWN

LEENIE B BOOKS
HALIFAX

No part of this book may be reproduced in any form, except in the case of brief quotations embodied in critical articles or reviews, without written permission from its publisher and author.

This book is a work of fiction. All names, events, and places are a product of this author's imagination. If any name, event and/or place did exist, it is purely by coincidence that it appears in this book.

No Other Choice © Leenie Brown. All Rights Reserved, except where otherwise noted.

Contents

Dedication vii

Chapter 1 1

Chapter 2 15

Chapter 3 31

Chapter 4 45

Chapter 5 61

Chapter 6 77

Chapter 7 93

Chapter 8 113

Chapter 9 131

Chapter 10 151

Chapter 11 171

Chapter 12 187

Acknowledgements 204
Choices Book Three: His Inconvenient Choice 206
Choices Book One: Her Father's Choice 218
A Leenie Brown Sampler 228

About the Author 259
Connect with Leenie Brown 261
You Might Also Enjoy... 262

Dedication

To all those who are neither the eldest nor the youngest but are lost in the middle

Chapter 1

DECEMBER 18, 1811

Lord Samuel Rycroft blinked and looked at his mother as if he was unable to understand what she had said. He took off his hat and placed it on the table in the entry way at Netherfield. "Pardon me?"

"I said we will depart for town when Miss Mary arrives." His mother made her way back into the sitting room and peered out the window. "There is no need to fear. She knows I am always early."

"I am still not understanding why we must wait for Miss Mary." He unbuttoned his great coat and began to shrug out of it. He had hoped to be in the carriage by now and on his way to town.

"Good morning, Georgiana," said Lady Sophia. "Did you have something to eat, my dear?"

"Yes, thank you." Georgiana laid her outerwear

on the settee with her aunt's things and took a seat near the window, so that she could see the drive. "I cannot wait for Miss Mary to arrive. It will be ever so pleasant to have her company."

"Company?" Rycroft's brows drew together. "Surely, we must not wait for you to finish a visit before leaving." He had things to do in town and a sister of Bingley's to avoid. He definitely did not have time for a social call.

Georgiana laughed. "A visit? At this time of the morning? I think not, Cousin. Miss Mary is to travel with us."

Lady Sophia sighed at her son's still puzzled expression. "She is coming to stay with me. Georgiana will soon be able to return to her brother, and I do not wish to be lonely." She smoothed her skirt over her legs. With her eyes lowered as they were she could not see his expression, which was her intent, but she could see his toe start to tap as the silence in the room grew. She looked up at him with a smile and then turned to look out the window.

"A project, Mother?" It was not unlike his mother to take on a less fortunate lady and help her to find a husband.

"No, no." She shook her head. "Miss Mary is not a project. She is a friend." She turned back to look at him. "I do like to have company of the female sort, and if that company happens to be a young lady of marriageable age and in need of some assistance, it makes me feel useful. It has been all arranged. Miss Mary will travel with us today and stay the week. We will visit the shops and arrange for her orders; then, she will return to Longbourn with her aunt and uncle for Christmas. She will rejoin us in the new year to participate in the season."

"A project." He ran his hands through his hair and shook his head. "And I am supposed to pay for this project?"

Lady Sophia crossed her arms. "Miss Mary is not a project. She is a friend and a guest of mine."

"Aunt," said Georgiana softly.

Rycroft sighed. "But you shall require me to attend all of the functions you select?"

"Well," said Lady Sophia, ignoring Georgiana's second soft call, "we shall need an escort, and you need to attend anyway if we ever expect to find you a wife."

"We do not need to find me a wife. I can do

that on my own." He hated being reminded of his duty to the title and his need to marry. He had been looking, but there were not any young ladies who interested him. They were all so agreeable, so biddable, so boring.

"You have done a poor job of it thus far, my son." Lady Sophia cocked her head to the side and gave him a stern look. "If you will remember, I gave you until this season to sort it out for yourself. Now, I will assist you. The deadline has passed for you to continue on without my interference."

"Fine." His eyes narrowed and his jaw clenched slightly. "I shall trot about with you and your project, Miss Mary, but I shall make my own decision." He stiffened as he heard a gasp from the doorway behind him.

"Miss Mary," Georgiana greeted Mary as excitedly as she could in an effort to counteract her cousin's words. "I have been anxiously awaiting your arrival."

Mary smiled as she always did when her father or mother or younger sisters said something insulting. It was not as if she was not well-prepared for handling such situations. "Good morning, Miss

Darcy, Lady Sophia, Lord Rycroft. My things are on their way with the carriage you sent, my lady."

Rycroft noted how her lips smiled, but her eyes held an ample amount of displeasure when she looked at him — which she did only briefly. Her words may have been pleasant, but he was certain her thoughts were not.

"Ah, Miss Mary, it is delightful to see you." Lady Sophia crossed the room to her. Placing an arm about Mary's shoulders, she said, "Please ignore my son. I am not sure where he gets his deplorable manners, for both his father and I did try to instill good ones in him." She cast a displeased look at Rycroft. "He likes to refer to any lady that I have taken under my care as a project. He thinks I am only interested in the hunt for a husband for the young lady, but I assure you, I am also interested in the gaining of many young friends and excellent connections."

Mary glanced at Rycroft, who was scowling slightly at his mother. "Perhaps, my lady, he needs to spend more time at church, so that he might learn to respect his parent, even if she is just a mother." This time, she did not attempt to veil the look of displeasure she gave him. "Or a bit of reading, perhaps, at night might suffice. I can give you recommendations if you wish." The smile returned to her lips, and her left brow rose just slightly.

"I do not need your recommendations. And I do attend church regularly." He pulled on his coat as his mother began to move toward the door with Mary. "And I do not appreciate being thought of as a man who does not respect his mother."

Mary halted and turned toward him. "Then, my lord, you should strive to make your actions match your beliefs, for at present they are quite contradictory."

"Quite right," agreed his mother, chuckling to herself at the look on her son's face. She was sure, had Mary been a man, there would have been a scuffle, for she had seen that look on several occasions before he and one of his cousins had engaged in a wrestling match.

Rycroft drew in a deep breath and released it as Georgiana took his arm. She looked up at him with a brow raised and a scolding look. "Do not," he said.

"Do not what?" She fluttered her lashes and smiled sweetly.

"You know very well, but since I must clarify,

do not chide me. I know I have insulted her once again and must apologize, although I doubt she will forgive me."

Georgiana hugged his arm tightly. "She will, if you are sincere. Miss Mary is quite agreeable and sweet."

Rycroft gave a soft short burst of laughter, unable to believe Georgiana's description of Mary. He had only seen her as scolding and scowling, but, he admitted to himself, he had not precisely given her reason to treat him well. He had, after all, said she was too studious in appearance and too serious to be of interest to him. He had not meant for the words to be a disparagement of her. He had been, in fact, disparaging himself. Although he was not precisely a slow learner, he had always been compared to his excessively diligent cousin, Fitzwilliam Darcy, and so the tease was meant to give Darcy a reason to chuckle at his cousin's expense. However, it had not gone as planned. Mary had heard his comment and taken offense, which in turn earned him a slight scolding from her sister, Elizabeth, and a lecture disguised as a story from Darcy. And for the last week and two days, he had done his best to mind his words and actions. He had even attempted to engage Mary in cordial conversation but to no avail. Although, she had readily accepted his apology, she seemed determined to avoid him whenever possible, and when that was not within the realm of possibilities, she often found opportunity to correct him for some small blunder. She really was a most frustrating young lady, and now he was to be in her company for the entirety of the season as her escort. He sighed. Perhaps his mother would magically transform the scolding and serious Miss Bennet into something more agreeable. If it were up to him, he would start by lightening the colours she wore and loosening the knot of hair on her head. It really did make her look entirely too studious and old, or at least older than he suspected she was.

He sighed once more as he saw Miss Bingley joining her brother in the hall to say their farewells. He had hoped that his mother's plan to leave quite early would have given him the opportunity to leave without speaking to Bingley's younger sister. She was just the sort of lady he tried to avoid — both cunning and simpering at the same time. He shook his head. It was beyond his understanding how any gentleman could be so easily taken in by the flutter of eyes and the strategic display of assets. Did they not realize that there needed to be a woman of substance behind the pretty face and tempting figure? That was not to say he had not enjoyed more than one tempting figure in his seasons. The thought brought a smile to his lips and kept him from rolling his eyes at Caroline Bingley's profusion of pleasantries to his mother. It did not escape his notice nor, he suspected, that of his mother, that she kept peeking in his direction to see if he was noticing the care she was paying to his mother. She was not the first lady to use such tactics. Perhaps if the good wishes and praise were sincere, it would have warmed his heart instead of causing him to wish to be elsewhere. He turned his eyes to where Bingley and Mary were speaking quietly.

"Mr. Bingley," Mary was saying, "should my father — "

"I will send word to Darcy and Rycroft immediately if there is any danger," said Bingley as he smiled and grasped Mary's hand, the one that was not dabbing her eyes with her handkerchief.

She nodded her head and her lips trembled slightly. "Thank you. I would not leave him, but he insisted. He kept saying he wished for me to go seek my happiness."

Bingley nodded and his face took on a serious expression, one which Rycroft had only seen on a few occasions. "He wishes to see his family secure. My father was the same when he became ill."

Mary nodded once again. "I know. He is thinking of when — " The handkerchief was once again near her eyes, and instead of continuing, she shrugged.

Bingley's expression returned to his engaging smile. "He is thinking if, not when. We must always hope."

Mary murmured another thank you and a final goodbye before moving toward the door.

"You will take care of her, will you not, Rycroft?" Bingley said as he watched Mary standing at the door waiting for the rest.

"No need to fear. My mother will have her well in hand, my friend."

Bingley drew Rycroft away from Georgiana and Caroline. "Lady Sophia will be able to help her with most things, but you have seen the books and heard the talk in clubs. I would hate to see her put upon by some schemer."

Rycroft nodded. He knew well of schemers, for he had been one at one time. "I have already been informed that it is my duty to escort my mother and Miss Mary to whatever events my mother chooses this season."

"Good," said Bingley. "I know Darcy will do his best to be of service to her, but ..."

Rycroft laughed. "Yes, he will likely be too occupied with his new wife to be present at many of his clubs."

Bingley smiled knowingly. "As will I, if things go well."

"So I shall be completely alone in my misery this season?"

"No, I shall still have to escort my sister, unless you would care to take her on as well?" Bingley laughed and slapped him on the shoulder.

Rycroft narrowed his eyes. "I do not have the patience of my cousin." He was unsure how Darcy had endured the fawning of Bingley's sister for all these years. She had been very persistent in making her desire to marry him known. He did his best to limit his exposure to the lady, insisting on meeting with Bingley only at a club or Rycroft Place.

Bingley nodded. "I have told her she has no hope, but she will not listen."

Rycroft sighed and rolled his eyes as Caroline came to where her brother was standing.

"Lord Rycroft," she began extending a hand to him.

He took it briefly and mumbled a hasty thank you and farewell before turning once again toward Bingley. "You will come around when you return to town, will you not?"

Bingley bit back a smile at the displeased look on Caroline's face."Certainly."

"Very good." He placed his hat on his head and gave a bow of his head to both Bingley and Caroline before walking to the door where he offered Mary his arm.

Mary lifted a brow, and he gave her his best pleading look to which she rolled her eyes and placed her hand on his arm. "I am sorry," he whispered as they walked down the steps to the carriage.

She nodded what he hoped was an acceptance of his apology. He made to hand her into the carriage, but she shook her head. "Your mother should be first."

He inclined his head. "Of course." He turned to his mother and then to Georgiana and finally to Mary before climbing into the carriage to take his place next to his mother. He leaned his head against the back of the carriage as it began to roll down the drive. Georgiana took out a small book and a pencil and began to draw. His mother took out a book and opened it to read. Mary also pulled out a book, but only held it on her lap under her hand which still held her handkerchief as she looked out the window. He saw her dab at her eyes and considered for the first time how difficult this must be for her. She must have noticed his observation, for her cheeks coloured slightly.

"I may be an oaf," he said, which caused her to smile quickly, "but I do understand the difficulty of not knowing..." his voice trailed off as he remembered having to return to school for his final term while his father was ill. He had been fortunate to have been able to return and spend time with him to learn of the responsibilities of the title. And then he had spent the next three years attempting to hide from the weight of that responsibility. He had tended to all the business involved, but he had spent an equal or greater amount of energy trying to lift the weight of the responsibilities by pursuing pleasure, a pursuit that had lead to his seclusion at his estate for the past six months while the gossip swirled and finally died.

Mary watched the emotions cross his face in the few moments of silence that followed and wondered at the cause for them. Perhaps he did possess a depth of thought. She smiled when he gave her a small shrug and a half smile. "Perhaps you are not a complete oaf," she said as she opened her book.

He laughed softly to himself. It was, he figured, the closest he was getting to a statement of forgiveness.

He tucked his blanket more securely around his legs, and then, tipping his hat to cover his eyes, he leaned his head against the back of the carriage and prepared to hasten the journey by drifting off to sleep.

Chapter 2

Mary sighed and flipped another page in Mrs. Havelston's book of patterns. "They are all lovely. I do not know what to choose." Her Aunt Gardiner had delivered the book of patterns to her at Rycroft Place. Mrs. Havelston did not lend her book to everyone, but Mr. Gardiner was a supplier of some very fine materials, and since he referred several customers to her, including his nieces, she was willing to lend the book to Mrs. Gardiner for an evening when needed.

"Surely, it cannot be so difficult." Rycroft took the book from Mary and placed it on the table where he had been playing cards with his mother while Georgiana and Mary had been looking at patterns. "What fabrics do you have?" Mary lay the samples on the table. "Your uncle has a good eye. These will all go quite nicely with your complexion, I dare say." He flipped through the book and placed a fabric sample between the pages when he found what he thought was an appropriate pattern. "How many patterns are you to pick for this order? Six was it?" He peered up from the page at her. "Very good," he said, turning his eyes back to the book when she nodded. "You will need gowns for driving, balls, and calls. You have a few acceptable day dresses now, do you not?" Again he peered up at her. Mary bit back a smile as she nodded. She had not seen another gentleman so interested in ladies' fashion besides her uncle, although, she suspected their interest was for very different reasons.

"There." He closed the book. "Now, might we have one more hand before we retire for the night?" He picked up the cards and began shuffling them. "Oh!" He lay the cards down and picked up the book again. "Do you ride?"

"A little."

He tilted his head to the side and raised a brow. "Georgie, we will have to improve that. All proper ladies must know how to ride." He flipped a few pages and scrutinized a few patterns before placing his finger on a picture. "That. In..." He studied her with eyes narrowed for a moment. "Green," he said at last. "Yes, a dark green. It will set off the auburn tones in your hair."

Mary looked at the book. The patterns he had chosen were very similar to what she might have chosen herself, although, they were a bit more daring than she would have considered. She smiled as she closed the book. She was in town to find a husband and to experience the freedom of not being pushed about by her mother and called upon to serve her younger sisters. She was not here to be the same old Mary, sitting by the wall and hidden in the background. No, she was here to see and be seen. The idea both thrilled and terrified her. But she was determined to be successful. She would not leave this season without a husband, or at least a glorious tale to tell to her nieces when she reached her spinsterhood.

She picked up her cards and arranged them in her hand. "You have a very keen eye for ladies' fashion."

Georgiana giggled. "He has a keen eye for ladies," she whispered.

Rycroft's eyes narrowed, and his lips curved

downward in a scowl. A most intimidating look thought Mary.

"I appreciate beauty and have an eye for quality." He lay his cards down on the table.

"It is not the quality ladies I worry about," said Lady Sophia.

A small hint of colour crept up Rycroft's neck, but he attempted to give her his most reassuring smile. "I am not the same man, Mother."

Lady Sophia patted his hand and smiled at him. "Time will tell, my son. Not that I doubt your resolve, but I do know the temptations."

He closed his eyes. Temptations were not something he wished to discuss with his mother, and definitely not with his cousin and Miss Mary. In fact, he had promised himself that he would avoid as many of the temptations that had led to his self-imposed exile as he could.

"I believe it is your turn, Georgiana," said Mary. She gave Rycroft a little smile when he peeked at her.

"Thank you," he mouthed, and she gave him a slight nod of her head in acknowledgement. To be honest, the fact that she had helped him avoid an embarrassing situation instead of taking the time to lecture him about his behaviour surprised him. But then, she was not from town, so perhaps she had not heard of the scandal.

Mary watched the play circle the table and come back to her. She was not sure why she had provided a way for Lord Rycroft to avoid the lecture she was sure his mother was about to give him, one she was certain he deserved. Perhaps it was because she knew what it was to have a mother embarrass her with a scolding remark. She played her turn. Perhaps it was because she felt she owed him a favour, having just been saved the task of making a decision about fashion. She did not mind speaking of fashion or admiring it, but she had very little knowledge on how to dress herself to advantage. Or, she sighed, perhaps it was because she had determined in the carriage ride from Hertfordshire that she would give him a chance to improve in her judgment.

"Lord Brownlow and Mr. Blackmoore to see you, sir," Morledge stood at the door.

"At this hour?" Rycroft placed his cards face down on the table.

"It appears so, sir." There was a hint of disapproval in the austere butler's tone.

"Very well. I suppose it would be the height of rudeness to send them away." One of his eyebrows rose, and his lips curled into a small smirk as he contemplated sending them away.

"If you are certain, sir." Morledge held his place.

"Yes, yes, show them in. I shall scold them for their inappropriate calling time or my mother shall." He winked at Mary. "Unless, of course, Miss Bennet, you would care to do the service."

Mary narrowed her eyes, and then that one eyebrow on the left rose a slight bit. "I am sure that is not how a lady makes a good first impression."

"Especially when the gentlemen are of the marriageable sort and very eligible, my dear. Brownlow has a title, but Blackmoore is not without his advantages. Quite plump in the pocket, they say." Lady Sophia gathered the cards and stacked them. "Georgiana, ring for tea. We will put on a good show."

"Mother," cautioned Rycroft, "they have come to see me, not Miss Mary."

"Of course, they are here for you and not Miss Mary. How can they be here for someone they have not met?" She smiled sweetly, but he knew that look. Perhaps he should be pitying Miss Mary more than himself for having to endure a season of his mother's scheming and matchmaking.

"Lord Brownlow and Mr. Blackmoore," Morledge announced.

Mary studied the men who entered. They seemed to be about the same age as Lord Rycroft and dressed in the current fashions just as he did. Neither was overly tall. In fact, she bit her lip for a moment and looked at Rycroft; they were both several inches shorter than he.

"Brownlow. Blackmoore." Rycroft greeted them.

"Rycroft," said the gentleman with the sandy hair and sparkling eyes, the one Mary thought looked very jovial. "We know it is late, but when we did not see you at our club this evening, we thought we should come here to welcome you back. It has been an age since we last saw you." Then, as if recognizing for the first time that there were others in the room, he bowed. "Lady Sophia, I trust you and Miss Darcy are well."

"We are quite well, Lord Brownlow. I thank you." She motioned toward some seats. "Please do sit down. I have sent for tea." She cocked her head slightly and gave them a smile. "Although I suspect, if you have been at your club all evening, you would do better with some coffee, but it is too late; the tea has been called, and we must make do." She raised a brow. "One must never waste tea. It is much too precious."

"Indeed, my lady," he said as he and Mr. Blackmoore each took a seat. "We had not intended to intrude on your evening, of course." He glanced at Miss Mary, who was sitting quietly observing the conversation.

"It is a pleasant intrusion. We were merely playing cards and speaking of fashion. I am certain my son is happy for the interruption." She looked at Rycroft and gave a tip of her head toward Mary.

"Yes, Miss Bennet is off to the modiste tomorrow, fashion catalogue in hand." He took a seat. "Miss Mary, this is Lord Brownlow," he motioned to the sandy-haired gentleman, "and Mr. Blackmoore," he motioned to the other gentleman. "Gentlemen, this is Miss Bennet of Hertfordshire. She is a guest of my mother for the season."

Chocolate. That was the colour of the other gentleman's hair. It was a lovely shade of chocolate that had been whisked with just a small amount of cream. "A pleasure to meet you, Lord Brownlow, Mr. Blackmoore." Mary smiled and nodded her greeting.

"Bennet?" It was the first word Mr. Blackmoore had spoken, and Mary quite liked the way her name fell from his lips. "Miss Darcy, did not your brother marry a Miss Bennet?"

"He did. He married Miss Mary's sister, Miss Elizabeth."

"Ah, a sister," said Mr. Blackmoore nodding his head. "And you are from Hertfordshire?" He turned his lovely brown eyes toward Mary.

"I am."

Rycroft was surprised by her demure tone and the slight blush that graced her cheeks. She was not the first young lady he had seen respond to Blackmoore in such a fashion, but he had not expected it of her, nor was he particularly pleased by it. "Her father owns the estate that neighbours the one Bingley has leased."

Mr. Blackmoore nodded again. "I hear Bingley has also found a potential bride."

"Another sister," said Mary. "My eldest sister, Jane. I have two who are younger than I as well. And no, I do not have a brother." It was what everyone asked and usually in a tone that spoke of their disapproval of such a thing as having so many girls and only girls.

Thankfully, at least to Rycroft, the tea arrived at that moment, and the subject of sisters and brides was forgotten, as talk turned toward the weather and the happenings in town. And when a proper amount of time had passed, and their teacups were empty, his mother, bless her, stood and excused herself as well as Miss Mary and Georgiana, citing Mary's early appointment with the modiste and the return of Georgiana's companion and the continuation of her lessons.

"She will take well," said Blackmoore after the ladies had departed. "That is why your mother has invited her to stay? Miss Bennet is her latest project."

Rycroft cringed. "That is what I called it, but my mother has assured me it is not. And I advise you not to use that term within her hearing."

Brownlow laughed. "She scolded you, did she?"

"Not as thoroughly as Miss Bennet did."

Brownlow's laughter increased. "You did not say that in front of Miss Bennet?"

Rycroft shrugged. "I did not know I had, but yes, I did."

"So she is a scolding sort of young lady?" asked Blackmoore.

Rycroft shook his head. "Not if you speak to Georgiana or Bingley or my mother or Darcy or, apparently, anyone but me. To them, Miss Mary is all sweetness, if a bit too serious, but to me she is more of a governess. I have been on the receiving end of more than one lecture." He closed his eyes and grimaced as he realized that the door had not opened to allow entrance to a servant to gather the tea tray. Turning, he saw Mary standing near the card table, the book of fashions in hand. Her cheeks were rosy, and her eyes were looking at the floor.

"I am sorry for the intrusion, my lord." She tried to keep the embarrassment and pain out of her voice. "I forgot my book, and your mother insisted that I return to get it."

"Very good," said Rycroft. "I....we...." He sought to find the right words to explain what she might have heard.

"No need to explain, my lord." She lifted her eyes and, with a small smile, curtseyed to the gentlemen. "Good night." She moved toward the door but stopped just before exiting and turned toward Rycroft. "I never lecture unless there is a want of learning." She curtseyed once again and left the room, closing the door firmly behind her.

She clasped the book tightly against her chest and took a few deep breaths. Then, having gained control of her emotions, she headed toward her room. Her resolve to give him that second chance crumbled with every step she took. Her anger at having been the subject of conversation, and in such a light, grew. By the time she had reached her room, her emotions were no longer under regulation, but the hurt she had felt at his words had been replaced by anger.

"Are you well?" Georgiana sat on Mary's bed, waiting for her.

Mary placed the book on the bed and closed the door. "No. Your cousin is a dolt." Mary flopped on the bed. "He was telling his friends that I am given to lecturing him." She sat up. "How shall I find a husband if he is labeling me a shrew? I would have a better chance of finding a husband with my mother standing about pointing out my sisters' accomplishments and my lack of them." She flopped back on the bed again.

Georgiana flipped open the book and began paging through it. She was unsure what to say to Mary. "He selected some very nice gowns."

Mary covered her face with her hands. "I cannot wear them."

Georgiana's brows drew together in confusion. "Why ever not? They are lovely and would complement you very well."

"But to wear what he selected? I will be constantly reminded of what he thinks of me."

"I apologize, Miss Mary, but I do not see how the two things are connected." She pursed her lips as she thought.

Mary uncovered her face. "I suppose you are right. They really are not related except for the fact that what he said was said by him and they were chosen by him."

"So, my cousin is the connection?" She looked at Mary, who nodded.

"But could you not use that connection to prove him wrong?" Mary lifted onto her elbows, interested to hear what Georgiana had to say. "What if you wore them and were the most unshrew-like lady ever? Would that not just prove to him that he may have known what would look best on you, but he knew nothing of who you were beneath the dress? You shall wear the dresses he chose and charm all the gentlemen with your sweetness, and Samuel will have to admit he was entirely wrong about you, which he is, of course. Men are not the brightest of creatures, you know. At least that is what Aunt Sophia says."

"That is simply brilliant!" Mary sat up and pulled the book closer, so that both she and Georgiana could look at the pages. "This one is very lovely."

"And you shall be the bell of the ball in it." Georgiana lowered her voice.

"Do you think Mr. Blackmoore will ask for a dance? He is very dashing, is he not?"

Mary sighed. "Very."

"Oh," Georgiana's hand covered her mouth, and her eyes sparkled. "That would be the very best way to prove my cousin wrong! You must convince his friends that he is wrong." She clapped her hands in excitement. "I so wish I could go to all the soirees with you. It is going to be so much fun."

Mary laughed. "I believe you are right, Georgiana. This could be a very entertaining project."

Chapter 3

Lord Rycroft rubbed his neck and then stretched. He had been bent over his account books for far too long. He needed a distraction. The letters and numbers were beginning to jumble themselves together. He pushed the account books away and stored his pen. Perhaps stretching his legs would be beneficial. The rain that beat against the window told him that his ramble would have to be confined to the house, and so he followed the notes of a lovely song to the music room, planning to slip into the room and sit quietly at the back while Georgiana practised. He was at the door with his hand on the handle when the voices from inside made him pause.

"No, no," said a strict voice. "The right foot, not the left one. Again. Watch Miss Bennet." The music began once again, and Rycroft pushed the door open just a bit to see Mary and Georgiana standing up to dance with each other.

"You know they could progress much more quickly if they had proper partners," Lady Sophia whispered behind him causing him to jump and rattle the door.

"There is only one of me and two of them," he retorted.

"The dancing master is another," she pushed the door open and held it while she waited for him to enter. "It will not do you any harm to polish your steps before you begin your quest to dance your way into some young lady's heart."

He sighed. The music had stopped and the occupants of the room were not waiting patiently. They each wore a differing amount of irritation on their faces. He stepped across the threshold as Lady Sophia announced that he was there to be of assistance.

The dancing master gave his an appraising look. "Do you dance well?" he queried.

"I would like to think I do," replied Rycroft.

"A cotillion?"

"Of course."

"Very well," said the instructor with one last

appraising look. "Stand up opposite Miss Bennet. I shall stand with Miss Darcy. She is struggling to know her left foot from her right foot at the moment, but Miss Bennet only wants practice to refine her steps." He bestowed a nod and a smile on Mary.

"You dance well?" asked Rycroft as he took his place across from Mary and bowed.

"I would like to think I do." She curtseyed, looking very much like she wished to laugh at her repetition of his answer.

She had not scolded him once today. She had not even glared at him once today. He had been sure there would be some repercussions for his blunder last night. Truth be told, he would have felt better if she had scolded him. As it was, he was left feeling as foolish as he had last evening and a bit nervous not knowing exactly if she would at some moment feel the need to chastise him. She looked expectantly to the musician seated at the piano.

"So you like to dance?" Rycroft asked, feeling he need to fill the void. Moreover, if he could get her to speak to him, perhaps he would soon be given the reprimand he deserved and the gnawing of his conscience would subside.

She smiled at him, an eyebrow raised a bit in amusement. "I do," was all she said.

"Do you dance often?" He attempted again.

She bit the side of her mouth to keep from giggling. "Not so often as I would like." She looked once again at the musician who had just finished spreading her music on the instrument, preparing for the dance the instructor had requested. She was determined to avoid Lord Rycroft's presence as much as she was able, but if it was not possible to avoid him, and she knew complete avoidance would be impossible, she had determined to speak to him as little as possible. If she did not speak, she could not lecture, and if she did not observe him, there would be nothing about which to lecture. And so she kept her eyes averted to the piano.

He tipped his head to the side. "I see what you are at."

She fluttered her eyes and smiled sweetly at him. "I assure you I am at nothing."

"You are angry, and so you refuse to speak to me."

"I am sure I have not refused to speak. I believe

I have answered all your questions." The music began, and she took his hand and curtseyed as he bowed before taking Georgiana's hand and beginning to circle.

When she had crossed over and back toward him, he said, "But your answers have been abrupt, and you seem adverse to conversation."

She crossed over and back to him. "My answers were concise, for I am intent upon my lesson. Now, if you would be so kind as to allow me to concentrate on my steps and the music..." She gave a small nod of her head as if thanking him for his compliance as they parted and came back together again.

He continued progressing through the steps in silence, his stiff muscles relaxing and the activity bringing alertness to his mind. As he danced, he watched Mary. Her steps were precise and soft; her movements were graceful; and if he was not mistaken, he heard her softly humming the tune. The joy on her face gave further evidence that she did indeed enjoy dancing while her skills told him that she had danced often. It was a delightful picture, one that brought a smile to his lips. Soon the music slowed and came to an end.

"Much improved, Miss Darcy," said the dancing master.

"You can return in two days, can you not?" asked Lady Sophia. "Miss Mary's time to prepare for the season is limited."

The gentleman inclined his head. A smile crinkled the skin around his eyes. "I would return every day to dance with Miss Bennet, but I have other students, so I shall have to be content to wait two days before I return." He gave Lord Rycroft an appraising look. "It would do well if the ladies had an opportunity to practice once between now and our next lesson." He cocked his head to the side, and both brows rose as he waited for Lord Rycroft to respond.

"I have business—" he began, but a small cough from his mother stopped him. "but, I am certain I can find a few moments to be of assistance."

The instructor turned to Miss Darcy. "Do you have the music for the dances we did today?"

"I do."

"Then perhaps you could play for Miss Bennet and Lord Rycroft, and then Miss Bennet — you do play, Miss Bennet, do you not?" He waited for her assurance that she did play before continuing.

"Then you must play for Miss Darcy and Lord Rycroft." He gave a sharp nod of his head, indicating that the plan was good and the discussion at an end. Then, with a scold to the musician to be quick, he donned his hat and coat and took up his walking stick.

"You dance so very well," said Geogiana. "I wish I could do as well."

Mary put an arm around Georgiana's shoulders. "You will. I have had more practice is all."

Georgiana shook her head. "My feet do not always follow my head."

"That is the problem," said Lord Rycroft. "You must not dance in your head." He smiled as Mary rolled her eyes. Finally, he had gotten a response that was not prim or proper as all her others had been today. "You do not believe me, Miss Mary?"

His tone was teasing, which caused Mary to both bristle and become wary. It would be very easy to scold and reprimand if he were allowed to tease. So, instead of responding with an *I most definitely do not*, she said, "I await your explanation, sir." And then she gave him as sweet a smile as she could.

One of his brows rose slightly, and his mouth

became a displeased line instead of the tempting smile it had been. She was definitely playing at something. He had given her the chance to instruct him on the need to know the dance in one's head before it could become a learned pattern for the body, but she had not taken it. And now, he needed to explain something he was not sure he could explain. "Well," he began. "The steps must first be known by the head, of course, but," he glanced at the pianoforte and remembered how Georgiana seemed to flow along the keys with the music, "but it is the heart which must be engaged with the music, as it is when you play. Do you count the notes and timing?"

She shook her head. "I did at first but no longer."

"Ah." He smiled as he saw Mary's eyes narrow. He was certain she had hoped he would not have an explanation. "If you do not count, how is it that you can play as it is written?"

A smile spread across Georgiana's face. "My heart and body feel it."

"Just so." He tapped her on the nose. "Would you agree, Miss Mary?"

Her eyes narrowed just a bit more, and he smiled just a bit more broadly.

"I would." She moved toward the instrument. "However, sometimes, fingers and feet do not learn at the same rate. One may require more practice than the other." She took up a piece of music which lay on a bench near the pianoforte. "If you will excuse me," she looked at him and then toward the door, "my fingers do not learn as readily as my feet."

Instead of leaving as she had clearly signaled she wanted him to do, he pulled a chair close to where she took her seat at the instrument. "You may require assistance with the pages," he explained when she looked up at him with brows drawn close in question.

Her shoulders drooped a bit as she sighed. Avoiding Lord Rycroft was becoming a challenge. "I would not wish to keep you from your business."

He waved the idea way. "My business can wait. I have worked at it all morning and desire some time away from it." He leaned back in his chair a bit. "Was your trip to the modiste a success?"

"It was. Mrs. Havelston was impressed with your selections." She placed her fingers above the keys and gave him a smile. "Now, if you would be so kind as to allow me to concentrate on my music."

He nodded.

Mary's fingers began working their way through the song as Georgiana joined her companion, Mrs. Annsley, near the window to work on a sampler.

Lady Sophia, with a twinkle in her eye and a smile on her lips, took a seat near enough to her son to both see and hear what passed between him and Miss Mary. She had, from the moment she met Mary, considered her a good match for Samuel, and having watched the two interact, she was certain she was right. Samuel was not the sort to abide a silly or a biddable woman. He needed a lady who was determined, who had a quick wit, and who did not bow to his every whim. Mary was just the thing. She tapped her fingers on the arm of the chair as she contemplated just how to convince the pair that they were exactly what each other needed.

"You think too much," Lord Rycroft whispered as he moved a page.

"Shush." Mary shook her head. She had

promised herself she would not scold and yet, she had just done so.

"You do," he whispered again.

Mary's hands stopped, and she let the note fade into the air before turning to Lord Rycroft. "This is a new piece, and I cannot learn it properly if I do not think about what I am doing. And I cannot think about what I am doing if you insist on speaking to me."

He shook his head. "It is not entirely new. You played it when we were in Hertfordshire. I remember it." He settled back in his chair, a rather smug look upon his face. "And, I believe, my cousin spoke to you while you played."

"And I stumbled," said Mary. "I do not wish to stumble when called upon to exhibit during the season." She held out her hand for the sheet of music he held. "I must begin again."

He shook his head. "You do not need this." He placed the sheet on the floor next to his chair.

"Very well, I shall practice later." She began to rise from her seat.

"I shall not return it to you until you have attempted the song without it."

Mary's mouth hung open for a moment.

"You have only to sit and play badly to prove to me that you do not know the piece."

She sat once again and held her hands over the keys. "Have you not embarrassed me enough?" she asked softly. "Must you insist on continuing to do so?" She began to play. She stumbled once, and it was not fluid, but she managed to complete the portion of music he held ransom.

It was not a lecture or a scold, but it was what he had sought, an acknowledgment that he had hurt her. And as her soft words twisted in his heart, he had no idea why he had felt so compelled to hear it. He placed the page of music in line with the others and stood to leave. "I have deserved every one of your lectures and more." He gave her half a smile. "Remember, I am an oaf."

"Not a complete one," she replied with a small smile of her own.

He gave a bow and left the room.

Lady Sophia turned her attention to her book. Perhaps convincing them would not prove so difficult. She smiled as Mary began playing, and she noted the door to the music room open slightly. If the look on her son's face was any indication, he was half in love with Mary already although she suspected he did not know it.

Rycroft stood with the door open just enough so that he could see Mary. Her eyes were closed, and her face wore the same smile of pleasure it had during their dance. He had meant to spend only a moment watching. However, the fascination of seeing the emotions play across her face and seeing her body rise and fall with the notes held him there for so long that the final note was fading as he hurried to close the door softly so she would not discover him watching her. He shook his head, baffled by his response to her. He looked at the door that separated him from the music that had begun once again, and though he wished to push the door open once more, he removed his hand from the door handle and returned to his study.

Chapter 4

Knowing that Lord Rycroft had mentioned the previous evening that he would be riding in the morning, Mary entered the breakfast room the next morning without worrying about whether he would be there or not. She had managed a full day without once giving in to her desire to lecture, and he had seemed rather contrite in all his actions toward her after he left the music room. It was as if he was trying to prove to her that he was not the oaf he continually claimed to be. It was quite unsettling to have him behaving so well. It made it difficult for her to maintain her resolve to avoid him, for he was pleasant company. Relieved that the breakfast room was indeed all hers, she filled her cup with tea and began to toast her bread.

"Ah, good," said Rycroft as he entered the room. "Is Georgiana awake?"

"Are you not riding?" Mary turned her bread trying to focus on it rather than the man who was disturbing her quiet breakfast.

"I have, and I will." He took a piece of bread and placed it on a toasting fork before joining her at the hearth. "You said you did not ride well. We should remedy that."

"Today?" Mary's eyes grew wide in surprise, and she nearly forgot to turn her bread again.

He nodded. "Did you have other plans?"

"We are going to the museum to draw this afternoon, but I had no plans other than to practice or read this morning." And she had planned on avoiding him again today.

"Good." He placed his bread near hers. "Now, do you know if Georgiana is awake?"

Mary sighed and turned her bread one last time. "She is, but I do not have a riding habit, so I am afraid we will not be able to ride today."

"I thought of that. I have borrowed one from Brownlow's sister."

"You did what?" Mary pulled her bread from the fire and slid it off onto a plate. Apparently, avoidance of his lordship was not going to be an option today.

"I borrowed a habit."

"From a lady I have never met?" She hoped beyond hope that he had not painted her as a project in need of assistance.

"Is this a problem?" His brows were drawn together. "Lady Serena was happy to help."

Mary's knife stopped with the sweet cream only half spread on her toast. A knot formed in her stomach. "What did you tell her?"

"I said that my mother had a guest staying with her and that the lady would like to ride but, unfortunately, did not have a habit with her." He joined her at the table, his toast looking, in her opinion, a bit too sickly white to be proper. "I did not say anything that would embarrass you."

"Are you certain?"

He paused and his brows drew together again as he thought. Then, he nodded his head. "Yes, I believe everything I said was acceptable."

Relief washed over her as she cut her bread into small triangles. "Then, I thank you."

He blinked. He did not know what he had expected — more questioning perhaps or some other objection to his plans — but not a thank you.

"Is she a particular friend of yours or merely the sister of a friend?"

He was still looking at her mouth — the lips that had just thanked him — as she lifted a piece of bread and took a bite. He quickly shifted his gaze to his plate as the tip of her tongue flicked out to catch a small bit of jam that remained on her lips.

"Merely the sister of a friend. She is all but betrothed to Lord Bowthorpe. It is expected to be the match of the season, or so her mother says." He peeked up at her just as she kissed a bit of something from the tip of her finger. He expelled a breath and returned his attention to his own toast and the topic of conversation. "I believe, however, your sister's conquest of my cousin may eclipse it for a time."

At that, Mary giggled. The thought of her sister Elizabeth being the talk of the ton was strange. "If I had to choose a sister to be the topic of gossip, I would not have chosen Elizabeth." She shrugged. "Kitty, possibly. Lydia," she sighed, "more than likely."

"And you?" There really was something about her eyes when she was amused, a twinkle that was most becoming.

"It is not one of my goals," she said with a laugh. "But if the gossip were for a good reason, which it rarely is, I would not be adverse to being a small topic of conversation."

"And what would you say is a good reason?" He filled his cup with tea.

"I do not know. Something noble. Something of significance to help another. "

He laid his spoon on his saucer and lifting his cup and stared at some object across the room. "Even when an act is done for all the right reasons, the gossips have a way of twisting it about to make it scandalous. They do not want to hear of good or noble acts." He shook his head. "They do not deal in the imparting of truth or kindness." There was a hint of bitterness in his voice. "And they enjoy nothing better than to ruin the life of any young lady who makes an error." He took a sip of his tea.

Mary chewed her last bite slowly and swallowed, washing it down with the last of her tea. "That is what happened to you," she said softly.

He looked at her in surprise. "You heard?"

She shrugged. "Papa read the news. Lydia read the on dit, and I listened." She stood to leave. "Do not fear. I shall not ask. You may be a partial oaf, but I do not believe you are what the gossips portrayed."

He grabbed her hand as she moved to leave. "You do not wish to know?"

She smiled at him. "I did not say that. I said I would not ask."

He dropped her hand. "Thank you. That you, an acquaintance of short duration and a lady of principle, would not label me as they do means a great deal and to do so without knowing the full story means even more." She stood waiting for him to continue for he looked as if he would. "I was very much like the man they portrayed me to be. Reckless. Seeking pleasure. Shirking responsibility. But never to anyone's harm but my own."

Mary lay her hand on his. "As you told your mother, you are that man no longer?"

He smiled and nodded. "I hope that is true."

She gave him that little shrug again. "You must not hope. You must believe." She turned and walked to the door, but stopped. "The riding habit, is it in my room?"

"It is." He was still staring at that spot across the room. "Have Georgie join us in three-quarters of an hour."

He looked toward her, and she curtseyed quickly. "As you wish, my lord." His laugh followed her as she scooted out of the room. A smile formed on her lips of its own accord. Perhaps he was not so bad as she had thought. He had taken it upon himself to help her in learning to ride. As she ascended the stairs, she replayed his comments about the scandal that had driven him out of town. The emotions that had played across his face and found their way into his tone spoke of a man with more depth than she had considered. She had said she would not ask about the scandal, but oh how she wanted to! She remembered the story. She had looked for it in the stack of papers in her father's study after she had met him. Having matched him to the Lord R of Essex mentioned in the paper, she had read the information several times.

> *Lord R of Essex has made himself scarce from town after being found in the company of Miss F when he was known to have been courting Lady S. It is said that the jilted lady's brother, a close friend of Lord R, has broken ties with him.*

She stopped as she pushed open the door to her room and her gaze fell on the beautiful blue riding habit that lay on her bed. Lady S! Lady Serena? She turned and looked back down the stairs. He had said she was merely the sister of a friend, a friend who had looked nothing but pleased to see him when he had come to visit that evening. She walked to the bed and ran her hand over the fabric of the habit. Even when an act is done for all the right reasons, he had said. As she moved to the bell pull, Mary considered what right reasons there could be for jilting a lady, especially one who was presumably a friend. How she wished she had not made the promise to not ask him about the scandal! She rang the bell to have a maid help her change. Then, remembering her promise to tell Georgiana about being ready, she hurried down the hall to her door, watching over her shoulder in case the maid arrive before she returned to her room.

"Miss Darcy," she called. She bit her lip and stared at the open door to her room; anxiety that she would cause the made she had called to wait climbed her spine, making it prickle. Thankfully, Georgiana was quick in opening the door. "We are to go riding with Lord Rycroft in three-quarters of an hour."

Mary looked over her shoulder and saw the

maid just reaching her room. "Oh, I must go. I forgot that I was to tell you of the riding until after I pulled the bell for the maid to help me with my riding habit." She was hurrying down the hall. "Well, actually, it is not my habit, it is borrowed."

Georgiana followed her. "Borrowed?"

"Yes," said Mary as she reached her room. "Lord Rycroft borrowed it from Lord Brownlow's sister."

Georgiana's eyes grew wide. "Lady Serena?"

Mary nodded.

Georgiana sat on the bed. "I did not think she would have lent him anything after what happened."

Mary stepped out of her day gown. "So she is the Lady S who was jilted?"

Georgiana nodded. "I did not think it strange that her brother would visit my cousin because a sister being attached to an equally worthy gentleman, who from all appearances is loved by her and loves her in return, is just the happy balm needed to heal a breach such as that." She sighed. "Men are such fickle creatures. But a woman who has been so injured?" She shook her head. "How does one recover from such a thing so fully and in such a short time?" She stood at the window looking out across the garden. "I am sure I could not," she said softly.

"Love heals," said Mary. "You said she loves Lord Bowthorpe, and he loves her?"

Georgiana nodded as she turned toward Mary. "Oh, Miss Mary! You look lovely."

Mary fastened the closures on the jacket. "It is a beautiful dress, and it fits so well."

"That it does," said Georgiana motioning for Mary to turn. "You shall not have to ride well to be noticed in this dress." She grabbed Mary's hand. "Come. Bring your hat. I will have my maid fix your hair once I am dressed." Georgiana pulled her down the hall towards her room. "You must tell me what you meant by love healing while I am dressing, Miss Mary."

Mary entered Georgiana's room. "Might you call me just Mary?"

Georgiana smiled. "If you will call me either Georgiana or Georgie."

"Very well," said Mary sitting on the bed. "Georgiana. It is a beautiful name."

"Thank you."

Georgiana's maid, who had just finished helping her dress when Mary had arrived to tell Georgiana they would be riding, had laid out her mistress's riding habit and set about helping her change as soon as the door had been closed.

"Now, that thing about love healing."

Mary cocked her head to the side and studied Georgiana. She seemed very anxious to hear this. Her expression was one of eager anticipation.

"My theory," said Mary, "and it is only a theory because I do not know the full story, is that there was either no attachment or a false attachment. Perhaps there was an infatuation between Lord Rycroft and the lady. Such sentiments are easily replaced by true and steady affection, which is a healing balm that wraps itself around your heart until the cracks and pain gradually fade away, and its steadfastness frees your heart to trust once again."

"What a beautiful thought," said Georgiana with a sigh. "Have you ever felt you were in love only to find your heart had tricked you?"

Mary smiled. "What young girl has not?"

Georgiana, fully gowned in her habit, motioned for Mary to sit in front of the mirror.

"Have you ever considered doing something very foolish because of those feelings?"

Mary noted the hint of pink that crept into Georgiana's cheeks. "I have, but I was prevented." Georgiana's maid had removed the pins from Mary's hair, and it tumbled down her back nearly to her waist. "I was to meet a young gentleman alone." She looked at Georgiana and then the maid.

"Oh, Sarah is very discreet," said Georgiana. "She will not share what she hears."

"No, miss. What I hear stays with me, miss." She had plaited Mary's hair and was beginning to pin it up securely in loops.

"Very well. I shall trust you." She gave Sarah a smile in the mirror. "I was fifteen and our neighbour's cousins came for the summer. One cousin in particular was of interest to me. He had just passed his eighteenth birthday. He was tall and had lovely blond hair that curled about his ears and at his neck and on his forehead." She sighed. "He was very handsome, and instead of paying any attention to my sisters Jane or Elizabeth, he chose to spend his time with me." As Sarah pinned her hat in place, Mary turned so that she could see Georgiana. "I had not ever had the attention of such a gentleman before Roger. He was amiable and charming. He was all that I thought a young man should be, but he was not as he appeared." She stood and allowed Georgiana to take her turn at the mirror.

"He read me poems and said very pretty things, and soon I fancied myself in love with him. I was so convinced of my feelings that I agreed to meet him on a walk. He had often whispered his desire to hold my hand and to kiss me.

"I blush to say that his constant attentions, his small brushes of his hand against my arm or the tucking of a stray strand of hair behind my ear, had left me desiring his kisses. I slipped out of the house on the day we were to meet a few moments earlier than necessary. I have never been given to tardiness, and it is what saved me. For as I approached the gate where we were to meet, I saw a bonnet duck behind a bush. He had been waiting for me with another. I saw them embracing. His hands were roaming over her back and..." Her cheeks coloured, and she dropped her eyes, "lower."

Georgiana's eyes grew wide with understanding. "How dreadful!"

Mary nodded. "I felt a fool for having fallen for such a man."

Georgiana stood with her hands on her hips. "But he was a deceiver! You could not have known."

"I should have known when he chose me over my sisters," Mary said quietly.

"Why?"

Mary smiled sadly at Georgiana. How did one explain one's lack of beauty?

"Oh, no!" said Georgiana. "Stand here." She pointed to a spot in front of the mirror. "I do not know what you looked like then, but look at yourself now. You are beautiful. Your cheeks are perfectly rosy. Your nose is small. Your eyes shine with your emotions, and your mouth is lovely — neither too thick nor too thin. And your figure..." Georgiana studied Mary for a moment. "Although you are not tall, your height is by no means deficient, and you have — Oh, I do not know how to say it politely — you have softness in all the proper places. You shall turn many heads this season, and one of them may possess that healing love of which you spoke."

Mary's cheeks were glowing quite rosy, and she had to blink against the tears that had formed in her eyes. "Thank you," she whispered. "I have never before heard myself described as anything so pleasant."

Georgiana wrapped her arms around Mary from behind. "You are everything that is pleasant. Is she not, Sarah?"

"That she is ,Miss. Always polite and very pretty." She ducked her head a bit. "I should not say it, but I heard it mentioned by a footman or two that you were pretty. They did not say it in an improper way, mind you. It was merely a comment made in passing about your arrival."

Mary smiled at Sarah, who was looking uneasy about having shared so much. "Thank you. That is very nice to hear."

"Did you require anything else, Miss Darcy?"

Georgiana looked at her reflection in the mirror. "No. You have done an excellent job. I dare say we are both very well-turned-out." She took Mary by the arm. "Shall we go present ourselves to our escort and instructor?"

Mary took a last look in the mirror, turning just a bit to inspect her complete outfit. It did fit well, and the style Sarah had created for her hair gave a softness to her features that she quite enjoyed. She smiled at her reflection and nodded her head. She was ready.

Chapter 5

Rycroft stood at the foot of the steps to Darcy House. The knocker was not on the door just as he had suspected it would not be, but knocker or no knocker, he was going to seek admission. And so he mounted the steps and gave a good loud rap on the door. He stood and waited for a count of ten before rapping once again. Another count of ten passed, and again he knocked. Finally, the door opened.

"Ah, Daniels, before you tell me that my cousin is not home to callers and close the door in my face — treatment that I know I well deserve, coming to call so soon after his wedding — let me assure you that I would not have called if I were not in dire need of his assistance." He put up his hand to stop the butler from replying. "A paper and pen would suffice. If I could just leave a message?"

Daniels gave Rycroft a most disapproving look but stepped to the side. "Please wait here. Mr. Darcy is currently in a meeting, I shall see if he is willing to speak with you after he has finished."

Rycroft's brows rose. "A meeting?"

"Yes," replied the butler. "It seems you are not the only person to ignore propriety today."

Rycroft shifted from foot to foot as he waited for Daniels to return. He was not even sure why he was here. He just knew he needed to speak to someone about that riding lesson. He shook his head to clear the images of Mary in that riding habit from his mind. He did not remember Lady Serena ever looking so enticing when wearing that gown. And he was not the only gentleman to notice how lovely she looked. They had been stopped by several of his acquaintances. They had made a show of welcoming him back to town, but the way their eyes wandered to Mary, he knew their real intent was an introduction. He had been particularly put out when Brownlow and Blackmoore had joined them. Both Mary and Georgiana had found the company of Blackmoore to be to their liking. He had even seen Mary ducking her head and blushing for the fool! He smacked his hat on his leg. The anger that bubbled now in his chest was most disconcerting. Blackmoore was a friend, so why had he wished to run the man off?

"The master will see you."

Rycroft followed Daniels to Darcy's study. He had not seen anyone leave the room. He smiled to himself. Perhaps the meeting had been with Mrs. Darcy? He stepped into the room as Daniels announced him. Mrs. Darcy sat in one of the chairs in front of Darcy's desk while Bingley sat in the other.

"Bingley!" Rycroft crossed the room and shook Bingley's hand. "You said you would call when you returned to town. Should I expect you later?"

Bingley laughed. "You should."

Rycroft looked at the faces of each of the room's occupants. "It is not dire news that you bring, is it?"

"No, no. My news is of the best sort. Miss Bennet has agreed to marry me. I have written to my solicitor about the license and papers, and I am in town for a few days as I finalize things. Miss Bennet has come to stay with her aunt and uncle, so I am here to let Mrs. Darcy know of her sister's arrival and to invite her and her husband to join us for the wedding." Bingley's smile grew as he spoke. "How is Miss Mary?"

"Miss Mary?" parroted Darcy, looking at first toward Bingley and then, Rycroft.

"She is well." Rycroft felt a bit of heat beginning to creep up his neck. It was an odd reaction. He had not blushed in years. "I have been compelled by my mother to assist Miss Mary and Georgiana with their dancing lessons."

"Mary is taking dancing lessons with Georgiana?" Elizabeth looked at the men in confusion.

"Forgive me," said Rycroft. "My mother has arranged for Miss Mary to join her for the season. Miss Mary is to stay with us until the end of the week. Then she will return to Longbourn for Christmas before coming back to Rycroft Place after the new year."

"And you are to escort them to all their soirees?" questioned Darcy.

"I am." Rycroft sighed. "My mother is intent upon finding me a bride this season, so I have no choice but to attend anyway."

Bingley laughed as he stood. "I do hope you are as successful as Darcy and I have been." He bowed to Elizabeth. "It has been a pleasure to see you, Mrs. Darcy."

"Now," said Darcy as Bingley moved toward the door. "What is your business, Rycroft? I had not intended to spend the whole of my day in my study."

Rycroft nearly laughed as he saw Elizabeth, her cheeks glowing rosy, duck her head and smile. "Yes, I am sorry to intrude, but I needed some advice."

"And it could not wait or be obtained from any other source?"

Rycroft shook his head. "I am afraid not."

"Very well," Darcy motioned to the chair Bingley had just vacated. "We will be in Hertfordshire the day before Christmas, Bingley," he called as Bingley reached the door.

Bingley gave a nod of his head. "Your rooms shall be waiting."

"Now, Rycroft," said Darcy as Bingley closed the door, "what can I do for you?"

Rycroft cast an uneasy glance in Elizabeth's direction. "It is of a private nature," he said softly as that infernal blush deepened.

"I am not home to visitors for I am spending

my day with my wife." Darcy smiled as he said the word, and for a brief moment, Rycroft felt a small jolt of envy which surprised him nearly as much as his anger had earlier today. "If you wish to speak to me, you must also speak to Mrs. Darcy."

Rycroft shifted uneasily in his chair. "It involves a lady." His ears were burning so greatly that he wished to cover them with his hands in an attempt to cool them.

"Very good." Darcy sat back in his chair, a look of enjoyment on his face. "My wife is a lady. She may be of assistance."

"I mean no disrespect, but I do not think so."

Darcy's brows rose, and his smile grew. He was definitely enjoying this. "Then, we have an impasse, for I shall not be parted from my wife today."

Rycroft blew out a breath. "Very well, if you insist." He shifted again in his chair. "There is a lady of my acquaintance who seems to have a very peculiar and disturbing effect on me." From the corner of his eye, he saw Elizabeth motion toward the door with her head, but Darcy shook his, and she remained seated. "I find myself seeking out opportunities to be in her presence, even when I know she is going to disagree with me or wish me to leave. And today, when we were out riding, I wished to run off a friend because she seemed to favour his attentions. And," he swallowed and spoke softly, "her beauty…" He raised his eyebrows but did not finish. "Why? What is wrong with me and how do I fix it?"

Darcy's smile had grown quite wide. "And if someone were to threaten her?" Darcy chuckled. "You do not need to tell me. I can tell by your look of horror that you would do whatever you needed to protect her. Correct?"

Rycroft nodded. "What do I do?"

Darcy looked at Elizabeth. "You marry her."

Rycroft was sure his heart had stopped beating at the statement. "Marry her?"

Darcy nodded. "It sounds to me as if you are in love with the lady, and I find myself a great proponent of marriage these days."

Rycroft had risen and was pacing the room. "In love?"

"Yes, Cousin, in love. It is not such a horrible place to be."

Rycroft shook his head. "No, I have simply been out of town for too long."

Darcy laughed. "There were no ladies in the country?"

Rycroft shot him a look of displeasure. "None to my liking. Very grasping."

"Ah, unlike the ladies of the ton."

Rycroft did not miss the note of sarcasm in Darcy's voice. "I cannot marry her."

"And why is that? Inferior standing?"

Rycroft rolled his eyes. "She is not titled, but she is a gentleman's daughter, not that standing is of great importance to me, as you well know. She would make a fine countess."

"Is she married?"

"No."

"Betrothed?"

"No."

"Has she been so tainted by scandal that your standing would suffer?"

"No."

"Then, I really do not see a reason why you cannot marry her," said Darcy.

Rycroft huffed and folded his arms across his chest. "I cannot marry her because she does not like me."

Elizabeth laughed. "Might I suggest you employ

the use of a library at a ball and a loud aunt who loves to gossip. Then she shall have to marry you whether she likes you or not."

Rycroft looked at Elizabeth in horror.

"I jest at my husband's expense, my lord," she explained. "He has told you of our betrothal has he not?"

Rycroft nodded. "But you like him."

"Yes, now, but I did not know that when we were first betrothed. At that time, I thought I did not like him." She rose and walked behind the desk to stand at Darcy's side. "Fortunately, I like him quite well now."

Darcy put an arm around her and pulled her close to him. "Yes, fortunately," he muttered. "Perhaps if Elizabeth met her —."

"No." The word was said so quickly and with so much force that it startled both Darcy and Elizabeth. "Not that there is anything wrong with Mrs. Darcy, of course." Rycroft moved toward the door. "I am not ... it would not be... I cannot," he stammered and shook his head. He stopped with his hand on the door handle. "I shall let you return to your day. I do apologize once again for the inconvenience." The door was nearly closed when he popped his head back into the room. "Thank you."

"Will he be alright?" asked Elizabeth after the door closed. "He seemed rather shaken."

Darcy tugged her onto his lap. "It is not easy for a man to realize he is in love with a woman. It can be very unsettling." He kissed her neck. "A man likes to be in charge of things, and when his heart decides it is no longer going to be under his regulation, his mind often rebels." He kissed her just behind her ear. "But, when the mind finally yields and allows the heart to lead, and when the lady is no longer set against the gentleman, the results, though still unsettling, are quite nice." He kissed her lips. "Deliciously unsettling."

She placed a hand on both sides of his face. "Before I allow you to be deliciously unsettled, sir. You are saying no harm will come to him in his current state."

Darcy smiled. "That I cannot guarantee, but I can guarantee that if he allows his head to listen to his heart, he will find happiness. But, for now, we must let him struggle with it. It is not something we can do for him."

"You are certain?"

Darcy nodded.

Elizabeth leaned close to his ear. "Then lock the door, my dear husband."

~*~*~*~*~*~

Freshly dressed and having had a small beverage to fortify his topsy-turvy emotions, Rycroft stood outside the door to the sitting room at his home, ready to escort his mother, his cousin and Miss Mary to the museum. He felt he was ready until he heard what sounded to be Blackmoore's voice coming from the sitting room. Rycroft stood for a moment, listening to the conversation. His brows rose as he heard Blackmoore mention a desire to visit the museum with the ladies.

"Ah," said Lady Sophia, "Samuel is to escort us, but he might enjoy your company."

Rycroft straightened the sleeves of his jacket, took a deep breath, and entered the room. "Whose company might I enjoy, Mother?" He bent to kiss her cheek.

"Blackmoore's." She noted how carefully her son held his face expressionless as if trying to contain some emotion that he did not wish for anyone to know about. It was a good sign in her mind. Perhaps having a gentleman showing interest in Mary would cause him to see her in a different light, or should he already have found her of interest, it might cause him to act. "He has expressed an interest in attending the museum with us, and I thought since the ladies will be drawing, you might find it less tiring to be waiting about if you were to have a companion. The two of you could get lost in the exhibits for an hour or so while Mary and Georgiana draw, and then afterwards you might show us some of the exhibits you found particularly interesting."

"An excellent idea. What say you, Blackmoore? Care to traipse about the museum with me? Or shall we bring our drawing pad and join the ladies?"

Blackmoore laughed. "And have my drawings stand beside yours? I think not."

"You draw?" Mary's voice held not a little surprise.

"Some. Diagrams, maps, those sorts of things."

"So no sculptures or nature?"

"I am afraid not." He gave her a sad smile. It was a pastime he had enjoyed as a young man.

"I should be very sad to have to give up drawing things of beauty," said Georgiana.

Rycroft cocked his head to the side and gave his cousin a lopsided grin. "A diagram cannot be a thing of beauty?"

"That is not what I meant," protested Georgiana. "I meant I should hate to give up drawing objects whose very purpose is to be beautiful."

"Such as a flower?" He raised an eyebrow.

"Yes. No." Georgiana huffed. "I know what you shall do. You shall tell me that although a flower is a thing of beauty, it may also have a purpose such as to produce fruit and, therefore, food." She turned to Mary. "It is what he constantly does to me. He twists my words. He says he does it in an attempt to make me consider them more carefully."

Mary's left brow rose most enchantingly, or so Rycroft thought. "I would have to agree that to consider one's words is a most important skill."

He held her gaze for a moment. "Only an oaf would not," he said with a tip of his head in acknowledgement that he knew what she implied with her comment.

"Or a partial one," she added with a smile.

"Very true." He could not help the smile that he wore. Indeed, he wished to chuckle, but instead he made a sweeping motion toward the door and said,

"Shall we?" He only grimaced slightly when Blackmoore offered his arm to Mary.

It was a small grimace, just a slight twitching of the eyes and a flinch of the lips, but it did not go unnoticed by his mother, who had been watching the exchange between her son and Mary with great interest. She would not, of course, make mention of it. She knew that her son needed time to process things, which usually meant activity. He was not one to think while sitting still for hours, at least not when the thinking required the wrestling of conflicting thoughts. She smiled. Perhaps that is why he had gone for a third ride after escorting Mary and Georgiana home earlier. She took his arm. "I trust your ride was refreshing."

His eyes shifted from where they were watching Mary and Blackmoore to his mother. "Yes, most refreshing." He said the words she expected to hear, but in truth, he was anything but refreshed. His ride, which had included that visit to Darcy, had left him with more to ponder than it relieved.

He had returned with a determination to fulfill his duties as an escort for his mother and her charges, but he would bury himself in his work for the next three days until Mary had left; then he would take his ease until she returned. He hoped that when she left, his unruly mind would finally be able to set itself to right. It was merely the presence of an attractive female in his home which had him at sixes and sevens. Surely it was nothing more. With the return of Mary and the beginning of the season with its numerous debutantes and other hopefuls, he would find his attentions drawn to various ladies, and this feeling of one's entire existence being dependent on the acceptance of one lady would be just an unsettling memory.

He averted his eyes from Mary once again as Blackmoore handed her into the carriage. He dared not watch, for the overwhelming urge to remove the man from her presence was once again growing as it had earlier during their ride.

Three days. Just three days, he reminded himself. In three days, Mary would be safely away from Blackmoore's attentions and his own heart would be safely returned to a state of calm, of being securely under his regulation once again.

Chapter 6

Mary tipped her head and studied the statue before beginning the work of completing the fine details of her drawing.

"Mr. Blackmoore is very handsome," whispered Georgiana, who was seated next to her. "And I do believe he has taken a fancy to you." There was a great deal of excitement in her voice.

Mary smiled. "I should not be disappointed if you were correct." She began shading her drawing, giving it depth. "He is handsome and seems polite, but I know very little of his character." She held her pencil still and looked at Georgiana. "And, as I have learned, character is of far greater importance than pleasant features and flattering words." She sighed. "It is not impossible for the two to coexist, for I believe they do in your brother and Mr. Bingley, but I admit to remaining wary when it is my heart which is in danger of being hurt again."

Georgiana bit her lip as images of a handsome and flattering man crossed her mind, a man who had convinced her that she was in love with him, but whose character was revealed to be as unattractive as his face was handsome and his words were pleasing. Her heart ached at the thought of how she had been so ill-used and the hurt and concern she had caused her brother due to her foolishness. "I cannot fault you for being cautious. You must not risk a second injury, but he is my cousin's friend. Surely there is something to be said in his favour because of that."

Mary considered that for a moment while she drew. She was not certain that a fact such as that was a mark in favour of Mr. Blackmoore's character. "I do not wish to offend, for I know Lord Rycroft is a beloved cousin, but it is my understanding that before he journeyed to the country, he was considered," she paused and looked around the room quickly, "somewhat of a rake," she whispered. Her cheeks flushed slightly at having spoken such a thing. "He has proclaimed he is not the same man, and I believe him, but does that not cause you to wonder about his friends?"

Georgiana laid her pencil down. "I had not thought of that, but surely one man is not guilty of all his friends have done just because he is their friend. Is he?"

"I believe a person must be careful not to judge another based only on supposition, but I also believe a person must be careful with whom they associate for not all are so careful in their casting of judgment." She sighed deeply. "By their fruits you will know them. That is what the good book says. We must watch their actions and deeds. How does he treat his mother, his sister, a friend, even his servants and animals? If he is harsh with them, you can know he will also be harsh with you. If he is too liberal with them, he may also be too liberal with his finances and the direction of his children, leading to ruin. Whose interests does he place first? Are they always his own? If they are, he will also place them before your interests and needs. There is so much to consider when accepting the attentions of a gentleman. It is quite daunting, but our lives and happiness depend upon careful consideration of all things." She smiled at Georgiana. "I do apologize. I am given to moralizing. It is something about which my sisters have often chided me."

Georgiana looked at her thoughtfully. "I do not see anything wrong with instruction."

Mary laughed. "That is because you have not been subjected to my admonishments as frequently as they have. However, I am attempting to learn to lecture only when necessary, but I do find it hard not to state my opinion when provoked."

Lady Sophia, who had joined them, chuckled. "I would venture to guess that such is the struggle of all intelligent females. What are we discussing?"

"The many things which need to be considered when accepting the attentions of a gentleman," said Georgiana.

"Indeed?" Lady Sophia's brows rose in surprise. She had not thought the two young ladies had been engaged in quite so serious a discussion, but it pleased her that they were. Her niece needed a friend who could help her in such areas. It was all well and good that Georgiana had Mrs. Ainsley and herself as guides, but she knew to have a woman of similar age discuss the topic would carry far more weight. "And what is on your list of considerations?"

"Character demonstrated through actions." Georgiana beamed like a pupil who had been called upon and knew the correct answer.

Again Lady Sophia could not help but be impressed with the conversation the two young ladies had been having. "Mrs. Ainsley and I have been admiring the exhibits. There is a fine collection of jewelry that might be of interest when you have completed your drawings."

Mrs. Ainsley and Lady Sophia took another turn about the room as Mary and Georgiana continued their work. They had only been working for a short period of time when they were again interrupted.

"Oh, Miss Darcy! It is a pleasure to see you." Caroline Bingley, followed by two other ladies, stopped in front of where Georgiana and Mary were drawing.

"Miss Bingley." Georgiana's tone was polite but not overly warm. "I had not thought you were in town."

Miss Bingley waved the thought away. "My brother had some business, and I just could not bear to spend even a few days alone in the country."

"Were your sister and her husband not there?" asked Georgiana in surprise.

"Yes, yes, Louisa and Hurst actually chose to remain in the country, although I do not know why." She glanced at Mary, giving her a brief nod of acknowledgement, and then turned back to Georgiana. "I missed my friends ever so much. There is so very little to do in the country."

"I look forward each year to when I can return to the country," said Georgiana. "Indeed, I prefer it to town. Solitude pleases me."

"Oh, to be sure, seclusion in such a place as Pemberley must be refreshing, but Netherfield and the surrounding area are so unrefined."

"I did not find it to be so," said Georgiana gathering her things and rising. "We were about to take a stroll around the exhibits."

"As were we," said Miss Ivison. "What fun it would be to view them together."

"Such a large group?" said Miss Pearce.
"Yes," said Miss Ivison, giving her friend a nudge with her elbow.

"You know that does sound rather pleasant," said Miss Pearce.

Mary fought the urge to roll her eyes. "Is your brother in town for long, Miss Bingley?"

Miss Bingley gave her a look that said she found Mary's company not to her liking. "Three days. He has some documents to gather from his solicitor. Why they could not wait until after the new year, I do not know."

"But if he had waited, would that not mean you would have missed this opportunity to visit with your friends?" Mary linked arms with Georgiana.

Miss Bingley did not answer, but she slipped her arm through Georgiana's other arm. "Miss Darcy, when you have your come out, you will then understand more fully the attractions of town. The balls and soirees are so diverting. It is fortunate that Hurst and Louisa insist upon returning for the season. I would simply perish if I were forced to spend the season in the country."

"We understand you have an aversion to the country," muttered Mary.

"You would not know the pleasures of a season in town, Miss Mary." Caroline's tone was cool. "If it were not for the charity of your sister's new relations, I dare say you would never have had the pleasure."

Mary felt the sting of the comment. "I am grateful for the invitation to join Lady Sophia for the season. Whether the season proves a pleasure or not remains to be seen. What one person deems enjoyment may not be to another's liking, and as you have already mentioned, I have not experienced a season in town, so I can neither agree nor disagree with your assessment of its pleasures." Mary gave Georgiana's arm a squeeze and whispered her desire to admire a particular statue as she removed her arm and walked away from the group.

"A season will be of little pleasure for one of her standing," Miss Ivison whispered rather loudly to Miss Pearce, who tittered in response. "I wonder if she likes libraries as much as her sister?"

Mary blinked against the tears.

"Are you well," asked Rycroft coming to stand beside her. She glanced at him and then looked around. "Blackmoore is not far behind me. He stopped to speak with some acquaintances. I promise you I did not abandon him." She looked at him in surprise. "I thought I should tell you so that you would not feel the need to instruct me on duty to a friend."

Mary opened her mouth to retort but closed it again as she saw the lopsided grin he wore.

"Forgive me. I had hoped to take your mind off whatever or whoever has upset you. Perhaps my choice of topic was not the best, but what can one expect from an oaf?" He offered her his arm.

"Partial oaf, my lord." She placed her hand on his arm. "And, I am well." She sighed. She must learn to deal more effectively with ladies such as Miss Bingley. Was there a master for such lessons as there was for dancing, drawing and singing?

"If you wish such a lie to be convincing, you may wish to refrain from sighing next time," said Rycroft softly. "Those three are not worth the discomposure, I assure you."

She glanced up at him. "But, how does one bear their barbs with composure?" As she said it, the answer came to her, and she shook her head at her own lack of thought, for it was an obvious answer. "I know how."

"You do?"

She nodded. "I shall pretend they are my mother or my aunt or my younger sister. I have endured their comments for years. I shall smile and attempt to ignore them."

"Your mother and sister? They have been unkind to you?" The idea was surprising.

"Surely you noticed their treatment of me."

He remembered how Mary had been required to complete tasks for them and how her suggestions were often dismissed. He remembered her sitting quietly along the wall or in a corner while the others commanded the attention of all who were near. "They are like that all the time?"

She nodded. "Do not misunderstand me. I do love them, but they do not think before they speak."

"And they ignore you."

She laughed. "When I am so fortunate."

"Still," he said softly, "I am sorry you have been treated so."

"Thank you."

She smiled at him and the ache in his heart, which had started when he saw her standing by the statue alone and obviously distraught, began to lessen.

"Did you complete your drawing?"

She shook her head. "No. Miss Bingley arrived."

"Do you wish to finish it? I can sit with you."

His smile held a bit of something wicked in it. "That would certainly make Miss Bingley displeased."

Mary chuckled. "While it might be enjoyable to vex her, it might provoke her more than displease her."

"Very well, we shall continue our tour and try not to provoke the ire of Miss Bingley or her friends."

It proved impossible, however, to accomplish such a feat. Miss Bingley as well as Miss Ivison and Miss Pearce conveyed very well through their mannerisms and slighting comments just what they thought of Mary, and it was not difficult to read the displeasure in their eyes when Rycroft and Blackmoore paid greater attention to Mary than to any of them. So, when it was time to leave, Mary sank with relief onto the carriage seat.

"It becomes easier," said Lady Sophia gently. "Not all women in the ton are so small minded as those three."

"How do they ever expect to get husbands?" asked Georgiana in surprise.

Rycroft laughed. "They are not painful to look

upon, and they do each have a fortune. There are men who require little else."

"If I were a man," said Georgiana in indignation, "I am certain there would not be a fortune large enough nor a figure fine enough to tempt into marriage with a woman like that!"

Rycroft smirked. "If you were a man in need of fortune and an heir, you might indeed find yourself tempted." He put up a hand to stop her from retorting. "But, I agree. They offer nothing that would induce me to consider them either."

Georgiana crossed her arms and gave him a hard look. "And your friends? Do they agree with your way of thinking?"

Rycroft's eyes darted toward Mary. He was certain Georgiana was asking in regards to Blackmoore. "I cannot speak for the motivations of my friends, but I have never heard them mention any of those ladies in a favourable light. None needs a fortune, though all need an heir, and a few need to make a connection that will be acceptable to their fathers."

"Acceptable in what way?" asked Georgiana.

"That depends on the father, and it is not my place to say."

"If you cannot say, then how am I to know what a man finds acceptable in a woman? How does a lady secure a worthy husband if she does not know what men such as your friends find acceptable? Your friends are honorable, are they not?"

"As honorable as any man of failings can be." Rycroft shifted in his seat. It was not a comfortable topic for him to discuss, for his actions had not always been honorable, and he did know of some less than honorable activities in which a few of his friend partook. "I cannot speak to what all men want in a wife, for each man is as unique as each woman."

"Then, tell me what you will be looking for in a wife," Georgiana persisted.

"Yes," said Lady Sophia, "I should like to know what you consider necessary, so that I can help you find such a wife."

Rycroft groaned and rubbed his brow. "It is not an easy thing to put in a list."

"Try," said his mother.

"Very well, but I warn you it shall sound trite. I wish for a companion. That is all. I wish for a lady who is more than a lover and the mother of my children, someone who understands me and can converse with me, who shares my beliefs and opinions and is not afraid to challenge me when we disagree, but she does so with grace and kindness."

"What of her features?" asked Georgiana.

A bit of warmth crept up his neck. "I should think this is inappropriate to discuss."

"I find it perfectly acceptable in a lesson situation such as this. Do you not agree, Mrs. Ainsley?" said Lady Sophia.

"Indeed."

He darted a look toward Mary. "Of course, I would wish for a wife who is fair. One that is pretty if not beautiful. But truly, as much as this sounds like an answer given to placate, it is the character of the lady which shines through her words and actions that is most attractive; however, I do not wish to marry someone who is old and fat with warts and poor hygiene." He smiled. "Whatever other physical attributes I prefer, I shall not disclose." Again his eyes darted toward Mary. She was very different from the ladies he had courted in the past, and yet she drew his attention and engaged his whole being more than any had ever done. Three days, he told himself once again. Three days and then his heart and mind would once again be safely under his regulation.

Chapter 7

For the next three days, Rycroft attempted to keep to his study, but although his mind told him to focus on his business and to avoid his mother and her charge, his feet refused to obey. More often than not, he found himself sitting in the music room, listening to Mary play or in the sitting room reading a book and chuckling softly at her grumbles while she worked on some stitch that was trying her patience. And then there were the required dance practice and two more rides in the park. It had been a most enjoyable three days aside from the constant twisting of his heart and the ever-present growing dislike for Blackmoore, who had come to call on each and every one of those three days.

There had been the pleasant diversion of seeing Bingley and Jane along with her sister Kitty and Aunt Gardiner. It was Bingley who now stood at the door, instructing how the bags were to be transported. Rycroft stood to the side, listening to Kitty telling Georgiana about the gowns that Jane had ordered and the new one that she had been allowed to have made. He knew that Mary's order of dresses would be arriving soon and that the two that had arrived were safely packed into her trunk, for Georgiana had insisted that they be taken to Meryton and worn.

"I think everything is secured," said Bingley.

The unsettled feeling that had begun this morning when Rycroft saw Mary's trunk waiting near the door began to grow, and he thought for a moment he might cast up his accounts. It was just another of the inexplicable things he had endured in the past week. Taking Bingley by the arm, he led him down the hall a short distance. "Your sister," he began.

Bingley smiled broadly. "You would like to offer for her?"

"No." He said it so quickly and forcefully that Bingley could not help laughing.

"Then it is her behaviour that has caused an issue?"

"Not today," said Rycroft, "but the other day at the museum, she and her friends were quite unpleasant to Miss Mary."

Bingley sighed. "If you are worried that it will continue, I can assure you it will not matter the punishments I put in place."

Rycroft nodded. "I understand you cannot control her actions, but they caused Miss Mary to be distraught, and if you could perhaps just..." he paused and dropped his gaze to the floor "...perhaps just make sure she is not made too uncomfortable during your journey?"

Bingley's eyes grew wide, and he blinked several times. "Miss Mary?"

"She is a friend, and I am concerned for her. It is nothing more." At least that is what he was attempting to make himself believe.

"Of course." Bingley's smile and tone of voice spoke of his disbelief. "She will have her sisters as well as mine. All will be well."

"Right." Rycroft nodded. The information did nothing to relieve his growing unease, but he followed Bingley to the sitting room and made what he hoped was a good show of being delighted to have his home just a little less filled with ladies.

"Thank you," said Mary as she left the room. "You have been a very patient and gracious host."

He smiled. "Mostly. I did have a rough start."

"But you have improved."

"Do you not fear I will fall back into my oafish ways without your influence?" She laughed and assured him that she would return soon to correct any habits that insisted upon returning. He took her hand and tucked it into the crook of his arm to escort her to the carriage. It was only after they had reached the door that he remembered to remove his hand from covering hers.

He stood on the walkway for a good five minutes after the carriage had pulled away from the house. Then giving himself a bit of a shake, he asked for his horse to be readied. He needed a ride.

~*~*~*~*~

After an hour of riding, he was beginning to feel more steady, but he was not ready to go home. So, he sought out one of his clubs. A drink, a game, and some time in conversation with acquaintances seemed a good diversion.

"Rycroft," called a gentleman in a fine blue jacket. "We've not seen you in an age. Come back for another go at the marriage mart?" His golden curls bounced as he laughed. "I dare say you'll not have an easy go of it. The mamas will be wary of you."

"Endicott." Rycroft clapped the man on the shoulder and then took a seat across from him. "I am still an earl. There will be many who would turn a blind eye to many things to have their daughter become a countess." He thanked the server and took a long draw of his ale. "Not that I wish to be ensnared by a fortune hunter."

Endicott laughed again. "Not many do. However, if they are of the upstanding variety, Blackmoore is looking. Heard he has been courting some chit from the country who is in town for the season and staying with someone." He drummed his fingers on the table. "Never been good with names," he muttered.

Rycroft took another long draw from his tankard. "I believe the name for which you are searching is Lady Sophia Rycroft."

Endicott snapped his fingers. "That's it precisely. Well, then I guess I do not need to tell you about it." He leaned towards Rycroft. "Blackmoore says she is rather pretty. On the opposite side of tall but with a pleasing womanly figure." He winked at Rycroft.

Rycroft took one breath and then another as he reminded himself that it was not Endicott but Blackmoore who had been looking at Mary's figure. He knew that such a description was only the beginning of what Blackmoore would have said. He was not one for speaking with decorum when amongst his friends. It was something which had not bothered Rycroft until this moment. He placed his mug on the table and turned the handle a quarter turn towards himself. There was no reason for the action other than to keep his hands occupied. "He is not wrong."

"And she is staying with you?"

"With my mother and my cousin, Darcy's sister."

"Ah, heard Darcy got married." It was obvious that the beverage which Endicott was now enjoying was not his first.

"He did. It is his wife's sister who is staying with my mother."

Endicott's brows rose, and he pursed his lips as he nodded his head. "Makes sense then."

"What makes sense?" Rycroft felt a strange

foreboding. He was almost certain that what he was about to hear was not something he wished to know, but rather something he needed to know. He waved to the server and motioned to his mug. Another drink might be needed.

"Blackmoore has been blubbering these past three months about his inheritance being held for ransom. His father fears he will run the estate into the ground with his entertainments."

Rycroft's brows rose. "Entertainments?"

"Shortly after the whole incident with Brownlow that sent you running, he took up with an actress who fancies herself an excellent faro player, which she is not."

"I was not running from Brownlow. I was travelling with a friend."

Endicott laughed. "Of course the friend happened to be a very pretty young woman."

"She was in need of a ride. Ask Brownlow. Things were not as they were reported. Surely, you know how facts get manipulated to create a story." Rycroft finished his first drink. Endicott was a pleasant fellow, but he was not in possession of a quick wit when not drinking. When drink was involved, his abilities to reason decreased even further.

"Yes, yes, Brownlow said he was not calling you out and that you had done him a favour by leaving." He motioned to the server, but Rycroft pulled his hand down and called for tea.

"You are foxed, my friend," he said as Endicott began to complain. "Now, you were saying about Blackmoore?"

"Ah, yes, Blackmoore claims he loves this actress and wishes to marry her. His father is not in favour of such a union."

"Understandably. It would be a blight on the family reputation that would be hard to overcome, and Blackmoore has a younger sister who will be coming out this year."

Endicott nodded and attempted to put his finger on his nose, but it landed on his cheek. "Just so. His father had his will redrawn and threatened to cut him off completely unless he marries a lady who meets his father's approval. And, a connection to Darcy would be extremely acceptable to Blackmoore's father."

The sense of foreboding had grown to one of

dread. "He cares nothing for the lady he is courting then?"

Rycroft could hear the disgust in Endicott's laugh.

"A means to an end," said Endicott. "He will have his father's money, a pretty chit to bear him an heir and a mistress to occupy him when his wife is unavailable." He gave an angry huff. "The love of a woman can turn a man. Would have never expected such from him." He lapsed into a thoughtful silence as he sipped his tea and ate the biscuits Rycroft had ordered for him.

Rycroft also drank in silence. "Seen Brownlow today?" He needed to ask Brownlow about these facts. It was not that he did not believe Endicott. No, he was certain that what Endicott had related was true. He needed to know if Brownlow also knew of this, and if he would stand with him when he confronted Blackmoore.

Endicott shook his head. "No. Just you and Beaumont."

Rycroft drained his mug. "I had hoped to see him, so I will go in search of him."

Endicott waved him away. "Go. I will find my way out of here soon."

Rycroft stepped into the deepening shadows of a December afternoon. He mounted his horse and pulled his jacket a bit tighter as he made his way toward Brownlow's townhome, but seeing the knocker on Darcy's door, he altered his plans.

"If you will wait here," said Daniels showing Rycroft into the sitting room.

Rycroft took a seat in a chair with a high back and allowed his head to drop back against it. He rubbed his face and then covered his eyes with his hands. It was not late, but he suddenly felt very tired. His promise to Bingley to keep Mary safe from schemers kept repeating itself in his mind. Not only had he not succeeded, but he had also been the one to introduce the man to her. He sighed deeply. Blackmoore had been a good friend and although rather rakish, he had never before dallied with any proper lady's emotions.

"Are you well?" Elizabeth's question startled him.

He removed his hands from his eyes and rose to greet her. "A bit tired is all."

Elizabeth gave him a concerned look. "I find the shortness of the days at this time of year affects me, as does the desire to curl up before a warm fire on a cool day." She took a seat. "Darcy will not be long."

"Do you travel to Hertfordshire on the morrow?"

Elizabeth smiled. "We do. I admit to being anxious to see my father."

He looked out the window. "Bingley left today."

"Yes," said Elizabeth. "I did have a visit from Jane this morning. It was unfortunate that their departure was delayed so that they will have to travel in the darker part of the day. But, one cannot get married by special license without a license, so it could not be prevented."

"Bingley mentioned the delay when he arrived to get Miss Mary." Rycroft lapsed into silence.

Darcy gave Elizabeth's cheek a kiss and cast a wary look at Rycroft, who was still staring out the window. "Is he well?" he whispered.

Elizabeth shook her head. "He says he is merely tired, but I fear it is more."

"Rycroft," said Darcy crossing to where the man sat.

Rycroft rose and clasped Darcy's outstretched hand.

"Do you wish to speak here or in my study?"

Rycroft looked at Darcy and then Elizabeth. "You both should know."

He returned to his seat. "Blackmoore has been calling on Miss Mary this past week."

"An eligible gentleman?" asked Elizabeth.

"So he appears." There was a hint of bitterness in Rycroft's voice. He swallowed and held Darcy's gaze. "I have learned something of him that has left me at odds with myself. He was a friend, tried and true and, despite his eager pursuit of pleasure, honourable. I thought nothing of his attentions to Miss Mary. I did not doubt his intentions until now."

Darcy leaned forward. "What has happened?"

"Nothing yet." Rycroft shook his head. "But his intentions are not honourable."

"How do you know this?" asked Darcy.

"Endicott related to me how Blackmoore took up with an actress shortly after my departure from town. It is not a connection his father wishes to see move forward and, accordingly, strictures have been placed upon Blackmoore's inheritance." He drew a deep breath and expelled it. "He must marry someone who is acceptable to his father, and who could be more acceptable than a gentleman's daughter who has connections to you." Again he shook his head. "The marriage would only be to please his father. He has no intentions of giving up the actress."

Elizabeth gasped.

"I am sorry," said Rycroft. "I promised Bingley I would protect her from schemers, and yet, it is I who has brought this schemer to her." His jaw and fists clenched.

"And you wish to do harm to him," said Darcy quietly. "But he is a friend, and it feels wrong to think of harming him."

Rycroft nodded. "But what he has planned..."

"Is reprehensible. I understand far more than you know," said Darcy.

"You remember I was once friends with Wickham."

Again Rycroft nodded. "I know I must deal with Blackmoore, but what of Mary?"

"I shall speak to her," said Elizabeth. "Perhaps her affections have not been engaged."

Rycroft's shoulders relaxed as a weight lifted off them.

"You have not failed her."

Rycroft looked at Darcy in surprise.

Darcy gave him a wry smile. "As I said, I understand far more than you know. You have kept your promise to Bingley. Did you not hear of a scheme and take immediate steps to prevent harm?"

Darcy stood and Rycroft followed.

"Go home, Rycroft. Miss Mary shall be well. The most dire circumstances have been avoided."

Elizabeth took Rycroft's hat from the table and handed it to him as he reached the door. "Thank you," she said.

"For what?" he asked in surprise.

"For caring for my sister." She smiled at him. "You do care for her, do you not?"

Rycroft turned his hat in his hands. "Very much," he admitted. There was no denying it any longer. She had left, and instead of feeling relieved and his mind clearing and righting itself, he found that his world seemed to be lying at his feet in pieces.

Elizabeth laid a hand on his arm. "A library, an aunt, and a ball."

He chuckled despite his gloom. "If it becomes necessary, Mrs. Darcy. If it becomes necessary."

~*~*~*~*~*~

Mary opened her trunk and shook out one

dress and then another before hanging them in her wardrobe. It had been only a week, but it felt strange to be in her room listening to the chatter created by her mother and sisters. She sighed. She had not missed it. She preferred the quiet of Rycroft Place.

She saw the handkerchief Georgiana had attempted to tuck into her trunk as a surprise. She had embroidered a dark blue M on one corner and had put small yellow flowers on the other corners. Flowers she said Mary would have to see one day when she visited her at Pemberley. Mary ran a finger over the flowers. Georgiana was one of the many delights of Rycroft Place she was going to miss, for shortly after Mary returned to London, Georgiana was to return to her brother. Mary sighed. She had enjoyed their discussions. Some had gone far into the night. She tucked the handkerchief into her pocket and went back to her unpacking. She had nearly finished when her door was flung open, and Lydia skipped across the room and flopped on the bed.

"Was it very grand?" asked Lydia.

"Was what grand?" asked Mary.

"Rycroft Place, silly." Lydia clutched her hands

to her heart dramatically. "Did you meet any gentlemen that made you swoon?"

"May I come in?" Kitty stood at the doorway.

"Of course, you may come in," said Lydia before Mary could say a word.

Kitty looked to Mary, who nodded. "What was town like?" she asked softly.

Mary joined her sisters on the bed. She knew that she would not have a moment's peace if she did not answer Lydia's questions, although she doubted Lydia would be satisfied with any of her answers.

"Rycroft Place is very grand. It has many maids and footmen. The floors where you enter shine. And you would be able to stand four ladies side by side on the steps. There are three sitting rooms...not all on the same floor, and several bedrooms, a music room, a dining room, a library..."

"A ballroom?" asked Lydia, turning onto her stomach.

"Yes," said Mary.

Lydia sighed. "I should so love to have a ballroom. Then, I could dance and dance. Did you dance in it?"

"No," said Mary with a laugh, "but I did dance

in the music room. It is where Miss Darcy has her lessons."

Lydia sighed again, a loud sigh of longing. "I should love to have dancing lessons."

"I would, too," added Kitty.

"Was the dancing master horrible? Did he smell funny and have rotten teeth?"

Mary laughed again. "No, he was a gentleman of about five and forty. He had a funny way of speaking for he was not born in England. He was very direct, but he was pleasant."

"Did you dance with him?" asked Kitty.

"I did twice. The other times, I danced with Lord Rycroft, so the dancing master could help Miss Darcy through the new steps."

Lydia's sigh was wistful. "Lord Rycroft is handsome, is he not?"

"Most handsome," said Kitty with a sigh.

Mary nodded. She could not deny that she found him attractive.

Lydia propped herself up on her elbows. "I have heard he is a rake." There was excitement in her tone.

Mary shook her head. "He may have been, but he is not any longer. He is a very fine gentleman."

Lydia pouted. "So, he did not try to kiss you?"

"Kiss me?" Mary cried in surprise. "Why ever should he do that?"

"Because he is a rake and that is what rakes do. They kiss ladies."

"I told you," said Mary in a rather stern voice, "he is not a rake. He did nothing improper."

"Well, that is not at all amusing."

"Impropriety is not amusing. It is dangerous. It can lead to your ruin and that of your family."

Lydia rolled her eyes. "Did you go anywhere?"

"I went riding and to the museum. And there were a few trips to the modiste with Aunt and Lady Sophia. "

"Lady Sophia. How I should love to have such a name."

Mary shook her head at her sister's wistful tone. "Perhaps if you learn to be proper, you might catch the eye of a peer." She doubted that a peer would ever consider someone of their standing, but she knew the idea might induce her sister to at least attempt to learn propriety. She stood. "I should like a cup of tea before I retire." She wished to end the discussion before she had to admit to being called on each day by Mr. Blackmoore. She had enjoyed his attentions, but she did not miss him, not like she did Georgiana or Lady Sophia or, the thought startled her, Lord Rycroft.

Chapter 8

The following day, Mary waited outside the milliner's for her younger sisters to conclude their shopping. Shopping had never been a great pleasure of hers, but it was even less of one when her sisters squabbled over this lace and that ribbon. She drew in a deep breath of air and shivered. She prayed her sisters would be quick as she stamped her feet to warm them.

"Is there no room in the shop?"

Mary spun toward the familiar voice. "Colonel Fitzwilliam, what a delightful surprise! What brings you to Meryton?"

He shrugged. "My men."

Mary blinked. "Your men? This regiment is your regiment?"

He nodded. "I do not quarter with them in the winter, but I do check on them sporadically. I may detest my profession, but I will not disgrace it, nor will I have it disgrace me." His jaw was firmly set in displeasure.

"I fear some of the men have attempted to disgrace you?"

"No more than expected." He looked toward the shop. "Why are you standing here instead of inside where it is warm?"

"My sisters," said Mary with a sigh. "More precisely, Lydia. Kitty is not an issue, but Lydia lacks decorum. I came out here to find some peace."

Richard laughed. "The busy street is more peaceful than a shop with your sister inside?"

Mary nodded slowly, a small smile on her lips. "You have not met Lydia. She can fill a village with noise even if she is the only one in it." She could see her sisters moving toward the door as she spoke. "I do believe you are about to have the privilege."

Richard continued to chuckle as the door to the shop opened, and two young ladies exited. One was tall and, despite what he guessed was her young age, womanly in appearance while the other had features that were fine and delicate. He bowed as the two came to stand beside Mary. He was certain he knew which one was Lydia, for the girl, since setting foot outside the shop, had not ceased her litany of descriptions of the embellishments she had purchased for her bonnet, and he understood why a busy street might be a source of peace for Mary.

"Lydia," said Mary in a cajoling tone, "I am positively certain that you have made the most excellent choices in embellishments." The young girl stopped talking and suddenly turned her attention to the officer standing with Mary.

Richard's lips twitched as he tried to contain a smile at her flutter of lashes.

"Colonel Fitzwilliam, these are my sisters, Lydia, and Kitty..."

"Katherine," said Kitty softly.

Mary gave her a questioning look but corrected herself. "My sisters Lydia and Katherine, whom we call Kitty. Kitty, Lydia, this is Mr. Darcy's cousin, Colonel Fitzwilliam. It is his regiment that is quartered here for the winter."

"Miss Katherine, Miss Lydia, it is a pleasure to meet you." He tipped his head to each of them as they curtseyed.

"Your regiment." There was awe in Lydia's

tone. "Mr. Darcy did not tell us that this was your regiment. Oh!" She covered her mouth with her fingers. "Wickham did not mention you either."

"I imagine Lieutenant Wickham would rather forget me." His lips curled wickedly.

"Why ever would he wish to forget you?"

"Lydia," Mary scolded. She was certain the question had popped from Lydia's mouth without an even minuscule amount of thought.

"It is a fair question, Miss Lydia." He smiled at Mary, trying to reassure her that he was not in the least offended. "He has been assigned to my unit at my request. He owes me a particular debt of honour, one that I shall most easily see is paid with him under my charge."

"Oh, my, a debt of honour?" Lydia's hand rested on her heart, and for a moment, Mary thought she might swoon.

"His charms belie his character, Miss Lydia. I would be cautious in my dealings with him." The smile had faded from his face and a hardness had appeared in its place. "He is particularly not to be trusted with pretty young ladies such as yourself."

"He is a rake?"

Again Mary cringed at Lydia's inappropriate comments.

Richard shook his head. "The word is too good for him. Deceiver, seducer, blackguard are all more fitting."

Lydia's eyes grew wide. "Indeed?" She looked at her sisters. "This is very shocking. He seemed so obliging." She lifted her chin. "I for one shall not speak to him again, except perhaps to offer a greeting. It would be unspeakably rude not to at least greet him on meeting, would it not?" She turned her full attention on Mary.

"We should be kind even to our enemies," Mary instructed. "Kindness does not mean turning a blind eye to their characters, however. You would do well to be cautious."

Lydia nodded and spoke not a word. It was a reaction that surprised Mary. Lydia was not one to accept instruction so readily.

"We were about to walk home, Colonel. Did you wish to join us to meet our father?"

"I would indeed," replied the Colonel offering her his arm. "I should like very much to meet him."

~*~*~*~*~*~

Mary tapped softly on the door to her father's

study and waited for his call before pushing open the door. "Papa, we have a guest."

Her father peered over his spectacles at Colonel Fitzwilliam and motioned to the chairs in front of his desk. "I would stand to greet you, sir, but I fear if I did so, you may be required to pick me up off the floor when I toppled over." There was a lightness to his voice and a twinkle in his eye.

"Papa," scolded Mary. "You are not so ill as that."

He chuckled. "No, but it did sound better than admitting I am too tired to stand." He gave her a wink as she bent to kiss his cheek. "And who is your friend, Mary?"

"This is Colonel Fitzwilliam. It is his regiment which is stationed in Hertfordshire. He is Mr. Darcy's cousin." Mary stood beside her father as Richard stuck out his hand in greeting.

"Do you wish for tea, Papa?"

He tipped his head toward the cabinet on the right side of the study. "Port," he said. "Will you join me, Colonel?"

Richard acknowledged he would, and Mary began pouring the drinks.

"Did you have much trouble making your way

through my home while wearing such a fetching jacket?" Mr. Bennet tucked his blanket around his legs more tightly and leaned back in his chair. His book lay open on the desk in front of him.

"There was a bit of a flutter," said Richard with a chuckle, accepting a glass from Mary with a nod of thanks.

"A red coat can be a distraction with the ladies." Mr. Bennet smiled widely. "I spent a few years in one myself as many young men do. However, I cannot say I enjoyed it, aside from the attentions of the ladies and the opportunity to travel to another part of our great country." He steepled his fingers on his chest and rested his chin on them. "It also kept me away from my cousin. I was not so fortunate as you, Colonel. My cousin lacked a great deal of sense."

"I am fortunate in that way, I suppose," replied Richard. "Speaking of my cousin, we expect his company at Netherfield this evening."

Mr. Bennet grinned and took a sip of his drink. "Not one to be housed with your men?"

Richard shrugged. "Not when there is a more comfortable arrangement to be had."

"Smart man," said Mr. Bennet.

"Do you need anything else, Papa?" Mary asked.

"No, no. I am quite content. A good drink and a good conversation," he lifted his glass and tipped it toward Richard, "what more could be required?"

"Then, I shall return to Mama and my sisters," said Mary.

"Ah, she is a good girl," she heard her father say as she closed the door. She stood for a moment in the hall, her head leaned against the wall and a smile on her face.

"Are you well?" asked Jane.

"He said I was a good girl," Mary whispered.

"And you are," said Jane.

"But he has never said so before."

"You have not heard him say it," said Jane, "but I have. He gives praise sparsely."

"Save for you and Lizzy," said Mary. Jane allowed it to be so but beyond her understanding. Mary noted the letters Jane held in her hand. "For Papa?"

"One is." Jane held up the second letter. "This one is for you."

"For me?" Mary took the letter. Her brows furrowed. "I do not recognize the hand."

Jane waited impatiently as Mary broke the seal.

"Oh!" Mary's eyes grew wide as she scanned the message for the signature. "It is from Mr. Blackmoore." She folded it and handed it back to Jane. "I cannot accept this. It would be improper."

"What did it say?" asked Jane.

"I did not read it. I should not have it." Mary shook her head and wrapped her arms around her middle. A feeling of unease had begun to wash over her as she wondered if Mr. Blackmoore was another gentleman who would prove to have a character far less attractive than his features. "We are not betrothed. We are not even courting. He is merely a gentleman who is a friend and has called while I was in town. Give the letter to Papa, and please let him know that I did not read it. I cannot be forced to marry Mr. Blackmoore."

"He seemed amiable," said Jane.

"But a gentleman who writes a letter to a lady to whom he is not betrothed or courting shows very little care for the lady's reputation. A marriage to such a man would be a misery, I am sure." Tears had begun to slip down her cheeks.

"Come," said Jane taking her by the hand and leading her into her father's study. "Forgive me,

Papa, for my intrusion, but it is a matter of some urgency." She placed the letters on his desk and stood beside it with an arm around Mary's shoulders.

Mr. Bennet picked up the letters and noted the one that was opened.

"I did not read it, Papa." Mary's voice quivered just a bit. "I only looked at the signature."

Mr. Bennet's eyebrows furrowed as he saw the signature. "Mr. Blackmoore?" He lifted his eyes to Mary. "Do you know a Mr. Blackmoore?"

Mary nodded. "He called on me at Lady Sophia's house. He is a friend of Lord Rycroft."

"Ah," he placed the letter, unread, on the desk and picked up the second one. "I assume this is also from the gentleman." He broke the seal. "Is there anything I should know about him before I read this?" He peered over his glasses at his daughter who shook her head.

"I have told you all there is to tell, but I shall not have him. I shall not be tied to a man who thinks so little of a lady's reputation as to send her a letter without permission."

"May I?" asked Richard. "I know we have just

met, sir, but I would agree with Miss Mary's conclusion."

"You know him?" Mr. Bennet was unfolding the letter as he looked at Richard.

"Some, and what I know, while not utterly defamatory, is not flattering."

Mr. Bennet nodded and began to read the letter. "I assume," he said as he placed the letter on the desk, "that the one addressed to you is to ask you for a courtship. He has requested a meeting with myself if I should be agreeable." He quickly skimmed the letter addressed to Mary. "He certainly writes a pretty letter." He held it out to Mary, who shook her head in refusal. "So, am I agreeable to a meeting?"

"No, please, Papa."

"Is anyone else aware of the letters?" he asked Jane.

"Hill, but no one else."

"Very good, then, I shall consign them to the fire and write my refusal of the young man's request." He looked once again at Mary. "Is this what you wish?"

Her head bobbed up and down.

"Very well. It shall be done. Now, Jane, I think it

best if you take Mary to her room and allow her to recover." He raised a brow. "You must not let your mother know of this," he cautioned.

"We shall take the servants' stairs," said Jane with a smile.

~*~*~*~*~*~

Lord Rycroft sat in the sitting room with his mother and Georgiana. A book lay open on his lap and his fingers drummed a steady pattern on it as he stared out the window. He had stopped at Brownlow's house after his conversation with Darcy, but the man was out at a dinner party. He had left a message for Brownlow to call first thing in the morning. He checked the clock again and watched it for a moment to ensure that the hands were moving, for time seemed to be standing still.

"You seem anxious," said his mother.

He gave her a small smile and lifted his brows as he tipped his head to the side and shrugged slightly. She knew it was his way of saying she was right, but he was not willing to speak of it.

"It is rather dull without Mary," said Georgiana. "I wonder what she is doing. It must never be dull to live with so many sisters."

"Sisters can be pleasant, but they can also pose

problems," cautioned her aunt. "I have asked Darcy to stop here on his way out of town this morning. Mary's first ball gown has arrived, and she really must have it for the ball Bingley is planning."

Georgiana sighed. "It is so beautiful. I do wish I could see her in it."

"You will," said her aunt, "just not now."

Georgiana sighed once more and went back to her stitching.

Rycroft placed his book on the table and moved to the window. He wished he could see her in that gown as well. Georgiana was right. It was dull without Mary. He leaned against the window frame and fixed his gaze on the chair that Mary had occupied every morning for the past five days as she would stitch beside Georgiana. A sigh escaped him before he could catch it, drawing his mother's attention and causing him to turn once again toward the street. Finally, he saw Brownlow mounting the steps to his front door.

He straightened both his jacket and his posture. "I should like to see Darcy when he arrives," he said to his mother. "I will be in my study with Brownlow."

"Do you wish for tea?" asked his mother as he was about to exit the room.

"No, no. I have what we need."

She raised a disapproving eyebrow.

"It is but a short meeting requiring only a small drink." Her eyebrow lowered, but she still wore a scowl. "Truly, Mother." He stepped into the hall. "Brownlow." He motioned for his friend to follow him to his study.

"Your message sounded most urgent," said Brownlow as he took a seat and nodded his acceptance of a drink Rycroft was about to pour.

"I had an enlightening conversation with Endicott about Blackmoore." Rycroft handed a glass to his friend and turned to pour himself a glass. "What do you know of his keeping an actress in funds for gaming?"

Brownlow sipped his drink and glanced warily at Rycroft. Although the three of them, himself, Rycroft and Blackmoore, were known to have a good game with Endicott from time to time. Rycroft had always insisted on low stakes. Rycroft, the one friend everyone thought to be a notorious rake, was the most responsible of his lot. He refused to enter a gaming hell; he flirted with the ladies but rarely dallied beyond a few kisses; and he had only been truly foxed on a handful of occasions. It was why Brownlow had trusted him to play the part of suitor for his sister when the gentleman she favoured needed encouragement to step forward. "He was to end it before the beginning of the season."

Rycroft sat behind his desk. "So it is true?"

"That he has taken up with an actress? Yes." Brownlow swirled his drink, a sign he was not being forthcoming.

Rycroft placed his glass on the desk and leaned forward. "Endicott said that he had no intention of ending his relationship with this actress. In fact, according to Endicott, Blackmoore intends to marry a lady of sense and solid connections to appease his father and continue to keep the actress. Is this true?"

Brownlow nodded slowly.

Rycroft rose from his seat and paced to the window and back. "And Miss Mary is who he has chosen to pay such a price?" He leaned on the desk toward Brownlow. "No lady deserves such treatment."

Brownlow swallowed. "I know. I had hoped he

would truly be taken with Miss Bennet, and he would come to his senses, but he has not. And," he drained his glass and placed it on the desk, "and you must believe me when I say I have only just learned of this last evening. He has written to both Miss Bennet and her father requesting a meeting with her father and proposing a courtship to Miss Bennet."

Rycroft dropped into his chair, his heart sinking with him. "When? When did he write?"

"It was sent express yesterday."

Rycroft dropped his head into his hands. "I was entrusted with her protection from schemers."

"I had hoped..." Brownlow's voice trailed off as Rycroft lifted his head.

"I would have hoped the same," said Rycroft. "One does not expect his friend to take such a turn." He rose. "To lose her is one thing, but to have her so injured and nearly at my own hands." He shook his head. It was more than he could allow his mind to consider at the moment.

"Lose her?" Understanding began to dawn in Brownlow's eyes. "Ah, that is why you looked like you wished to call him out when we were riding the other day."

At that moment, Darcy entered the study. "Your mother said you wished to see me."

Rycroft motioned to the chair by his desk, but instead of joining Darcy and Brownlow there, he stuck his head into the hall and called for Morledge. "Have a bag packed quickly." He turned to Darcy. "You are at Netherfield for how many days?"

"The wedding is to be Tuesday next, and if the weather holds, we will return then."

"Pack enough for a week," he said to Morledge before turning his attention to Darcy and Brownlow. "Tell him of the letters," he said to Brownlow. "I must prepare to travel." He stuck his head back into the hallway. "My horse," he called to a footman. "Have my horse readied." He turned back to Darcy. "My bag and my man, may they travel with you?"

Darcy shrugged and nodded, unsure as to what was actually happening.

Rycroft clapped his hands once. "Good. I shall ride on ahead. She must not accept him." He spun and left the room.

Darcy looked at Brownlow in confusion. "About what is he babbling?"

Brownlow explained about the letters that had been sent the previous day. "He does not wish to either hurt or lose her," he concluded.

Darcy's brows rose. "So my wife was correct. He cares for Mary."

"So it seems," said Brownlow rising. "Now, he has not asked it, but I believe, I must warn Blackmoore of this development. I trust he is wise enough to know to step down, for if he does not, I fear he is risking far more than his inheritance."

Darcy chuckled and rubbed his jaw. "Not even I am willing to challenge Rycroft." He clapped Brownlow on the shoulder. "Come, you must at least give a word of greeting to Lady Sophia, and I believe you have not had the very good fortune of meeting my wife. Both of whom will find the reason for delaying my trip most diverting."

Chapter 9

Mrs. Phillips entered Longbourn's drawing room and greeted her sister and nieces before settling into a chair near Mrs. Bennet and beginning to share what she considered to be the best items of news. The butcher had been seen speaking with the baker, and this was just after the butcher's son had been seen walking with the baker's daughter. He had even offered her a ride on Sunday last. The parson's nose had been uncommonly red, and he had not been sneezing or sniffling. Lady Lucas was certain he had been indulging in spirits. So it continued for some time.

Mary did her best to ignore what was being said and applied herself to the dress she was mending. A low branch had caught her skirt on her walk this morning. It was naught but a small tear and easily repaired.

"I could not believe it, Sister," Aunt Phillips was saying, "but Mrs. Long insists that she had it from a most reliable source, though she would not tell me from whom she had heard it. But she was adamant that it was true." Mary saw her aunt look at her with a curious expression. "She says that Mary has been receiving letters from a gentleman and must secretly be betrothed."

Mary kept her eyes on her needle, not daring to look at her mother or aunt. A wave of unease caused her stomach to churn and her heart to race.

"It is true," said Lydia. "I heard Hill say there was a letter for Miss Mary. It came express." She leaned toward her aunt and whispered loudly, "From London."

Mrs. Bennet gasped, and Mary's face flushed while her head spun.

"Is this true?" asked Mrs. Bennet in a shrill voice.

Mary looked first at Jane and then her mother. "Is what true?" she asked cautiously.

"Are you secretly betrothed?"

"No."

It was her aunt's turn to gasp. "You are receiving letters from a gentleman, and you are not even betrothed?" She shook her head and clucked her tongue. "First, Lizzy and now, Mary. Sister, I am surprised you have not taught them better."

Mary watched her mother's eyes grow narrow and her cheeks become pink.

"It is not as it appears, Aunt," she said before her mother could begin to have a spell of nerves. "A gentleman has written to Papa requesting a courtship, but it has been denied. I could not tie myself to a man who would so blatantly snub propriety by writing to me without some sort of understanding. It would not be right, would it, Mama?"

Mrs. Bennet's mouth snapped shut, but she continued to look at Mary with surprise. "It most definitely would not." She tilted her head, and her brows drew together as she considered Mary as if she were a stranger.

Kitty turned from the window and her contemplation of the garden. "You refused him?"

Mary gave her a pleading look, hoping that she would not ask any further questions. "I did."

"Do you know who he is?" asked her aunt eagerly.

Kitty's eyes grew wide as she realized what she

had begun. She shook her head. "I do not know who has written to Mary." She bit her lip and ducked her head. "I only know she has had potential suitors call on her while in town." She peeked at Mary, who had her eyes closed and was looking a bit faint. "I could not begin to imagine who might have written with such a short acquaintance." She gave Mary a small smile and a wink when Mary opened her eyes. "But, with her new dresses and the hair style that Miss Darcy's maid has given her, not to mention the connections Lady Sophia must have, it would certainly be foolish for Mary to consider an offer so soon. Why," her voice rose to a level of excitement to match that of Lydia, "being the sister of a man such as Mr. Darcy and the particular friend of Lady Sophia and her son, Lord Rycroft, I would not be surprised in the least if Mary had several offers and perhaps even one from a peer."

Mary breathed a sigh of relief. Her mother and aunt seemed to be enthralled with such an idea and immediately began planning a wedding breakfast fit for a lord.

Kitty crossed the room and extended her hand to Mary and nodded toward the door. "I think a stroll before the sun sinks any lower would be most beneficial."

Mary gladly accepted the means of escape and taking her sister's hand hurried from the room.

"Was it Mr. Blackmoore?" asked Kitty. "I shall not tell a soul. I swear."

"It would not be right to say," said Mary, though she gave a small nod of her head.

"He is very handsome and wealthy," commented Kitty.

"He is," said Mary as she fastened her wrap around her shoulders. "But, I do not know his character, and we seemed to have very little in the way of common interests."

"How do you do it?" Kitty tugged Mary closer to her side. The air was decidedly cool, but the emptiness of the garden afforded the only real privacy to discuss such things. So, despite the shiver that shook her, she continued walking with Mary instead of retreating to the warmth of the house as she wished.

"I do not understand your meaning?"

"How do you make them like you?" She shivered once more. "Mr. Blackmoore, Lord Rycroft, Colonel Fitzwilliam. They all seem to be taken with you, yet you never bat your lashes or drop your gaze when you smile."

Mary was shocked to have such a question put to her. She had enjoyed the company of the three gentlemen mentioned, but other than Mr. Blackmoore's nearly fawning attention, she had never suspected any to have been interested in her as anything more than a person with whom to have a conversation. In fact, she was quite certain that Lord Rycroft found her presence to be somewhat of an inconvenience at best and a trial at worst. "They are friends, nothing more," said Mary.

"Friends?" said Kitty in disbelief. "I have seen the way Lord Rycroft watches you, and though I know only a little about men, I do not believe his look expressed mere friendship. He looked decidedly jealous of Mr. Blackmoore."

Mary laughed. "It is not possible."

"Why?" Kitty stopped walking and turned to face Mary. "How is it impossible for him to like you?"

Mary's smile was tight and the pain she tried to keep hidden was poorly concealed in her eyes. "I am not the sort of lady a man desires. I am bookish and opinionated, and I have very little to recommend me by way of looks."

Kitty's mouth hung open for a moment before she closed it and gave a shake of her head. "I own that you are opinionated, but little in the way of looks? That is a falsehood of the highest order. You may not put it on display very often, but you, my dear sister, are beautiful." She snuggled in again next to Mary as the wind tugged at her wrap and caused her to shiver once more. "False modesty is just as much a sin as vanity, is it not?" She laughed at Mary's small sound of shock. "I listen," she explained. "You are beautiful, and it is as you have admonished us to find, a beauty based not solely on the physical appearance but a beauty of character." She sighed. "But I do not know how to be like you. How do I find that beauty that inspires men to notice me?"

"Oh," cried Mary, "you should not try to be like me. You should be like you."

Kitty sighed. "But I am not interesting."

Mary laughed. "Neither am I, and yet you think there are three gentlemen who admire me."

Kitty giggled. "But you are smart."

"And you are talented. Your sketches are excellent, and your eye for detail will make you a marvelous hostess." She rubbed her hand up and down Kitty's arm that was twined with hers. "We should return before you catch a chill." Kitty suffered easily from chills and headaches. They were rarely serious, but feeling ill was not pleasant, and so Mary did not wish to place Kitty in danger.

"Do you," Kitty began as they turned back toward the house, "do you..." She took a breath and then spoke the rest of her question quickly, "find Colonel Fitzwilliam attractive?"

Mary patted her sister's arm, understanding what it was that she really wished to know. "He is handsome, but he is merely a friend." She leaned a bit closer as they were nearing the house, and she wished to keep her voice soft. "Do you find him attractive?"

Kitty nodded.

"I am glad," said Mary. "It would be a fine match for you, but he is a younger son and his inheritance is still under his father's control. So, I must caution you to guard your heart."

Kitty nodded again.

"He has but a year remaining before his father

will release some of what will come to him," said Mary.

Kitty pulled Mary to a stop. "You will not tell anyone that I prefer him?"

"No." Mary attempted to move toward the house once more, but Kitty held her in place.

"You have refused Mr. Blackmoore, and Colonel Fitzwilliam has not touched your heart. But what of Lord Rycroft?"

Mary sighed. "I do not know. He is good and kind and solicitous of my needs." She felt her cheeks warming despite the cold. "And he is very handsome."

Kitty smiled. "And he has come to call." She pointed toward the drive.

Mary looked where her sister had pointed. There, hat in hand, brushing off his coat, was Lord Rycroft. He, looking up at just that moment and catching her eye, smiled as he tilted his hat towards her before replacing it on his head and moving toward the front door.

~*~*~*~*~*~

Rycroft drew a deep breath and followed Mr. Hill down the hall to Mr. Bennet's study. He had attempted on his way from London to plan how he was going to present what he knew to Mary's father, but all his well-thought-out ideas had flown from his head when she had smiled at him and lifted her hand to give him a small wave as if she were glad to see him. Now, as he walked into Mr. Bennet's study, he tried to gather his thoughts.

"Lord Rycroft." Mr. Bennet rose from his chair with some difficulty and gave his guest a small bow.

Lord Rycroft returned the bow and waited until Mr. Bennet took his seat before sitting down himself.

"What brings you to call on me today." There was a twinkle in his eye. "I am sure you were not just in the neighbourhood, unless your sense of time and direction is sorely lacking."

Rycroft chuckled. "My sense of time and direction is normally accurate. I have come with a purpose. I have been made aware of some unsettling information in regards to a friend of mine and your daughter."

Mr. Bennet's brows rose.

"I assure you, it is only my friend who is at fault." He paused. "I do not know how to best tell you."

"I prefer the straight forward approach."

Rycroft nodded. "I have been made aware that my friend Mr. Blackmoore has picked up some unsavoury habits while I was out of town. His father is not pleased about his activities and has threatened to remove his inheritance unless he marries a lady who is acceptable to his father."

"Ah, that explains his letter wishing to court Mary." He watched as

Rycroft's jaw clenched and his head turned ever so slightly to the side as if the idea was something he found wholly unpleasant.

"He has no intention of giving up his habits after he marries." Rycroft again felt his jaw clenching as he tried desperately to keep his emotions under regulation. "If I had known of his activities and his attentions, I would not have allowed him in my home or introduced him to your daughter. I am sorry."

Mr. Bennet nodded and studied the face of the man before him. "I assume his habits include a woman?"

Rycroft nodded. "An actress with a fondness for gaming."

"It is my understanding that such affairs are not

unusual in the higher circles, of which I assume he is part."

The response surprised Rycroft and before he could think the better of his response, he had replied rather sharply. "Sir, we speak of your daughter."

Mr. Bennet smiled. "I am aware of that fact. I was merely wondering what your stance on such situations is. I take it from your response that you do not approve of such things?"

"I most certainly do not approve. A man is to take and keep a wife in good faith. To do otherwise is reprehensible."

"I am glad we are agreed." Mr. Bennet leaned back in his chair, a small smile played at his lips. "Mr. Blackmoore's offer was refused out of hand by myself and my daughter. She refused to even read his letter." His smile grew as he saw Rycroft's shoulders relax in relief. "However, you I would not refuse."

Rycroft's eyes grew wide. "I beg your pardon?"

"I approve of you," said Mr. Bennet. "If you should wish to court or marry my daughter, you have my blessing." He shifted in his chair a bit. "I may not have the luxury of time. I am still not well, so should anything happen to me before you can convince her of your worth and find yourself in need of my blessing, I am giving it now."

Rycroft shook his head. "You barely know me."

Mr. Bennet shrugged. "I know enough. Mary continues to count you as one of her friends, does she not?"

Rycroft's brows drew together. "I believe she does."

"Then I am satisfied." He winced slightly as he shifted again in his chair. "A letter containing the information you have shared would have sufficed as warning." Rycroft could hear the laughter that lay behind the statement. "I assume you would like to see my Mary."

Rycroft drew in a deep breath and released it. "I would, and I thank you for your approval."

"So you do care for her?"

"A great deal, sir." He stood and paced the length of the room.

Mr. Bennet chuckled. "It is an unsettling feeling at first. Sneaks up on a fellow. "

Rycroft smiled. "It does indeed."

Mr. Bennet's eyes shimmered. "Love her for who she is."

"I will."

"Very good." He dabbed at his eyes with his handkerchief and gave a shaky chuckle. "Before I become a watering pot, could I ask your assistance in walking to the sitting room? I find I tire of my books and actually wish to hear the noise of my family."

Lord Rycroft held out his arm to Mr. Bennet, who had once again, with some difficulty, risen.

"My strength has not returned. I fear the doctors may be right, and my days are numbered. But as Mary would says..."

"All our days are numbered," said Rycroft.

Mr. Bennet chuckled softly. "I see you know her well already."

"Papa," said Kitty as she descended the stairs on her way back to the sitting room, "are you to join us?" She dipped a curtsey in greeting to Rycroft.

"I am. Is Mary upstairs or in the sitting room?"

"I am here," said Mary coming from the back of the house. She smiled at Lord Rycroft, who nodded his head instead of bowing. "I knew Mama would be wishing for tea since Lord Rycroft is not the only visitor to have arrived. I saw Mr. Bingley's carriage from my window."

"Ah, well, it seems I shall soon discover if I have a place to sleep tonight." Lord Rycroft chuckled.

"Well, my lord, if Bingley will not receive you, Longbourn is not without guest rooms," said Mr. Bennet. "We would be honoured to do you the service."

"I shall bear that in mind." Rycroft leaned a bit closer to Mr. Bennet. "In fact, if Bingley's sister becomes too much of a trial, I may call upon your assistance."

Mr. Bennet chuckled. "Then, I should think we should arrange ourselves in the sitting room in such a way as to thwart her advances?"

"Just so, sir." Rycroft smiled and turned to Kitty and Mary. "Will you ladies be of assistance?"

Kitty wrapped her arms around Mary's arm. "We would be delighted, would we not, Mary?"

Mary's cheeks had taken on a light shade of pink causing Rycroft to wonder if she was irritated by the thought or if she were actually delighted.

"Of course." The response was quick as if said without a thought. Then Rycroft saw her give Kitty a small smile that seemed to contain a secret before she continued, "Perhaps Colonel Fitzwilliam could help as well. He is planning to call."

Kitty's eyes grew wide, and she darted an uneasy glance at Rycroft. "That would be lovely."

No, it would not be lovely, thought Rycroft — not if the secret smiles and looks between Mary and Kitty indicated what he feared . . . that his cousin had earned the place in Mary's heart that he desired for himself. But though is heart was sinking, he smiled and agreed before entering the sitting room, where after greeting Mrs. Bennet and her sister and then helping Mr. Bennet to a chair, he took a seat in a grouping of four chairs with Mary on his right.

Mary placed her hand on his arm for just a moment, drawing his attention to her. "I am glad to see you," she whispered.

"Are you as glad to see me as you are to see my cousin?" He tried to keep his tone light and teasing.

Mary's eyes did not leave his face as she considered just how happy she was to see him. She shook her head at the foolishness of missing someone so much when they had been apart for such a short time. A smile crept onto her lips. "My lord, as hard as it may be to believe, I have missed your taunting, so I believe I am more glad to see you than your cousin. The colonel is pleasing company, but he is far more polite than I have grown accustomed to in this past week."

Rycroft chuckled. "I do endeavour to be polite, but you are most provoking."

"I?" Mary laughed softly. "No, my lord, it is not I who is most provoking." She had raised her left eyebrow, and her eyes twinkled. It was an expression that he adored.

"You are too charming by half, Miss Mary," he said dryly.

She tipped her head as if acknowledging a great compliment. "Thank you, my lord."

Kitty coughed lightly and tipped her head toward the door where Richard was entering with the Bingleys.

Mary bit her lip and looked to Rycroft, "Could you draw his attention?"

"It is what you want?"

Rycroft's expression confused Mary. There was an uneasiness in his eyes and a slight furrow between his brows. "It is what we want." She emphasized the word we as she darted a look at Kitty. "Unless you would rather give the chair to Miss Bingley."

"Please." Kitty's plea was soft, her eyes imploring, and her cheeks rosy.

Rycroft smiled as understanding dawned on him. It was not Mary but her sister who wished the company of his cousin. "I would rather not encourage Miss Bingley," he said as he motioned for Richard to join them. He allowed his hand to brush Mary's arm as her chair was close enough to do so without being obvious. Although he knew his feelings for her, it would not do to let the rest of the room know before he had spoken to Mary.

The touch startled Mary in a most agreeable way. A slight shiver ran up her arm and down to her fingers. Her eyes were drawn to his face. The slight smile on his lips and the quick lifting and lowering of his brow told her that it had not been an accidental touch. The thought caused her heart to quicken and brought a smile to her face.

He leaned a bit closer to her and spoke softly so that only she could hear. "Miss Bingley has no hope with me, for my heart belongs to another." Once again he allowed his hand to brush her arm.

"I only hope I have a chance of success with the lady." There was a question not only in his voice but also his eyes.

Mary's eyes grew wide, and she opened her mouth to reply, though her mind was unsure of what she would say.

Rycroft shook his head. "I have shocked you, I am afraid. Please do not answer now. Just consider me."

"Of course." Mary nodded her head, which was swirling.

"Thank you," said Rycroft as he stood to clap his cousin on the shoulder before giving him a quick embrace.

Mary sat quietly for much of the conversation, listening intently to the interaction between the two cousins and watching the way Rycroft treated Kitty. Yes, he was handsome, titled, and wealthy — three things that all ladies longed for in a match, yet these qualities were not sufficient for her. As she continued her observation, her heart spoke to her of what she believed to be true. She was certain that, though it may not have always been true, he was now a man of good character, a man worthy of consideration. It would be a good match she decided, and with time and a bit of good fortune, perhaps she could grow to love him.

Chapter 10

Rycroft settled into a chair near the fire in Netherfield's drawing room and opened a book. He had made certain to draw the chair away from the others, separating himself, he hoped, from any possible conversations. He did not wish to discuss his reasons for travelling to Hertfordshire any longer, and he knew that Bingley and his sister, in particular, would not stop their questioning until they had gotten the full story. Apparently, the need to see Mr. Bennet and deliver some news was not reason enough to quell their curiosity. In fact, it seemed that it had only incited it. He sighed as he watched Darcy draw Bingley aside. Bingley listened intently to Darcy and then turned to look at him. Rycroft nodded. He was sure that the most trustworthy of the Bingley siblings now knew that Mary was his true reason for arriving unannounced.

He let his eyes fall to the page of his book, but his mind was not particularly interested in the words that the author had written. It was more pleasantly engaged in contemplating Mary. She had been surprised at first by his declaration, but her actions toward him did not seem to discourage his suit. In fact, she had eagerly agreed to his calling the next day.

"Sister," Caroline was saying in an exaggerated whisper. "What we heard today in the village is true."

Louisa gasped softly. "Indeed? Pray, how do you know?"

"Miss Lydia said that a letter was delivered to her sister, and the stable hand told Mrs. Phillips that the messenger was paid handsomely to ensure that news of the delivery was shared. It was from a wealthy gentleman in London."

"Is there a secret engagement?" asked Louisa, leaning eagerly toward her sister.

Rycroft held his breath as he waited for the reply.

"No." Caroline's tone was one of great disapproval "What lady accepts a letter from a lover without an understanding?"

Louisa sighed. "If you consider how her sister snared Mr. Darcy, you should not be surprised. It seems the Bennet ladies have a lack of scruples." She clucked her tongue and shook her head. "I do not know what Charles is thinking, tying himself to such a family."

Rycroft snapped his book closed and leveled a very displeased look at Bingley's sisters. "A lack of scruples?" He gave a short bitter laugh. "Unlike you who repeat tales as fact even though they were first told by a man paid to tell them? Not only do the two of you lack scruples, you quite obviously lack intelligence." He rose. "If you will excuse me, I would rather not have my reading disturbed by the babblings of a harpy." He spotted a chair in the opposite corner of the room and headed toward it.

Bingley sighed as he watched Rycroft obviously scold his sisters and find another chair. "I wish he had at least a small measure of your patience," he said to Darcy. "Do I apologize to him or speak to my sisters?"

Darcy chuckled. "I would not wish to speak with them at present. I do not believe I have ever seen them quite so displeased. His scolding must have been harsh indeed." He looked to where Elizabeth was sitting. She had taken a place that was removed from where he spoke with Bingley but was not too near Caroline or Louisa. He could tell that she had heard the exchange and was working hard to contain her emotions for her lower lip was between her teeth; her eyes blinked rapidly as if trying to contain tears, and her hands clutched her book tightly. Darcy cleared his throat, drawing her attention. Then, with a smile and small tip of his head called her to him.

"I believe my wife may be able to be of assistance." He took her hand and placed it between his. "Elizabeth, do you know what made my cousin so angry?"

"Gossip," she whispered.

He heard the waver in her voice and without a care for what others might say, pulled her closer to his side.

She glanced nervously behind her to where Caroline and Louisa sat.

"Do not worry about them," he said softly.

"You did not hear what they said," she replied. "Apparently, I snared you and due to the letter that was sent to Mary, we Bennet ladies are without scruples."

Darcy turned toward the sound of Richard's groan. "You know of this?"

Richard's brows drew together. "You know of it?"

"I know of a letter," he replied cautiously.

"She did not read it," said Richard. "She gave it to her father, and he read it. She did not even consider his offer."

"I do not know of this," said Bingley.

Darcy sighed. "Blackmoore offered a courtship. His plan is to marry her to please his father and keep his inheritance. But," he darted a glance toward Rycroft, "Rycroft learned that Blackmoore has no intention of breaking off his relationship with a particular actress. It is why he is here — to inform Mr. Bennet of Blackmoore's character."

"And, based on what I observed today, to court Miss Mary," said Richard.

Darcy shrugged. "Aye, that, too."

Bingley blew out a breath. "And my sister is displeased and attempting to discredit Miss Mary, but," his brows drew together, "how did she learn of the letter?"

"The messenger was paid to spread the news," said Rycroft, who had been watching the conversation and had come to join it, knowing full well it was about him.

"And my aunt was most willing to share the information." Elizabeth turned to Rycroft. "Does my sister know about Mr. Blackmoore?"

He shook his head. "I only spoke to your father."

"Then, I shall call on her first thing tomorrow while you gentlemen are off riding."

Darcy shook his head. "I will attend you."

"But my mother will be busy with preparations for the night's dinner."

"And your father will be pleased to hear something other than a female voice."

Elizabeth laughed. "That is very true, so you have my permission to attend me."

"Thank you, my dear," said Darcy. "Would you care to join me, Rycroft?"

"No, no. Miss Mary expects me later, and if I have learned one thing from my mother and your sister, it is that you do not surprise a lady outside of calling hours. It was quite the lengthy diatribe, but there was something in there about proper gowns and hair." He chuckled. "They did not appreciate my theory that such a call was most beneficial since a gentleman should know what he will see each morning."

This earned laughter from all who were gathered, but when it had died, Rycroft became serious once more. "Her reputation," he said.

"It may be tarnished for a time," said Elizabeth softly.

"And if I call on her or offer for her, will it make it better or worse?"

Elizabeth smiled as she watched him rub his hands in circles on his knees just as her husband did when nervous. "My aunt will assume that it was you who sent the letter and when she makes an assumption, it is not long before all of Meryton will know."

"So, I should not call on her?"

Elizabeth leaned towards him and placed a hand on his. "You should do what your heart tells you. Believe me when I say fighting it is not worth the battle." She gave his hand a pat. "She would not be the first Bennet lady to endure the whispers of Meryton." She tilted her head to the side and gave him a playful look. "Mr. Bingley is giving a ball, and he has a very nice library. One rumor is often forgotten when another is begun." This drew a laugh from them all.

"If it becomes necessary," said Rycroft as he rose. "I think I shall take my book to bed." He cast a look in Caroline's direction. "The door will be locked and a piece of furniture against it, so if there is an emergency during the night, you will need a couple of stout footmen to help you gain entrance."

Bingley chuckled. "I can have Hurst return to town earlier than planned."

"No," said Rycroft, "I should like her to witness her defeat." He smiled wryly. "I just pray I am successful."

~*~*~*~*~*~

Mary's mouth hung open, and she looked at her sister in disbelief. She could not believe that the intentions of Mr. Blackmoore had been so dishonorable.

"Lord Rycroft learned of it two days ago and immediately came to tell Mr. Darcy and me. And then when he learned of the letter that had been sent, he was on his horse and gone before a half hour had passed."

"Are all men so devious?" asked Mary.

"What do you mean?" asked Elizabeth.

"Do you remember Roger?"

Elizabeth nodded. "He seemed quite smitten with you."

"But he was not." She blew out a breath and fought the tears that gathered. "I slipped out to meet him one morning — it was the first time I had agreed to do so — and I arrived at our meeting place earlier than planned." A tear slid down her cheek. "He was there with someone else. I turned and ran and avoided him as best I could for the remainder of his stay in Hertfordshire."

Elizabeth gathered Mary into her arms. "And now, Mr. Blackmoore has done the same." She said it softly as she stroked Mary's hair. "Not all men are dishonorable. Papa, Mr. Darcy, Uncle Gardiner, Colonel Fitzwilliam, Mr. Bingley and..." she pulled back slightly to look into Mary's face, "and Lord Rycroft are all honorable men. They are not perfect for they are as human as we are, but they are trustworthy and good. And I believe Lord Rycroft is in love with you." She sat for some minutes with her arms wrapped around Mary and her chin resting on top of Mary's head. "Mary," she said at last, "how do you feel about Lord Rycroft?"

Mary sighed a long drawn out sigh that was obviously filled with confusion. "He is agreeable, even if he does vex me at times, and he is kind." She sighed again. "He does not know it, but I have seen him lend a hand to a footman who was struggling to move a piece of furniture. And all of his servants seem content and at ease. And Georgiana adores him and he, her. I believe she could ask for the moon, and he would attempt to get it for her." She tilted her head to see Elizabeth. "Papa seems to approve of him."

"A very good sign," said Elizabeth with a laugh, releasing Mary from her embrace.

Mary crossed the room to get a fresh handkerchief. As she did so, she passed the parcel that Elizabeth had brought. "Oh," she cried, "my gown! I had nearly forgotten you brought it." The handkerchief was forgotten for the moment as Mary opened the parcel and lifted the dress out with great care. "It is beautiful," she whispered as she held it up in front of her.

"It is," agreed Elizabeth. "The detail is lovely." She ran a finger gently over the small red roses that adorned the neckline and sleeves of the cream coloured material. There were more rose embellishments at the hem and a frothy ruffle that made the dress seem as if it was rising from a cloud. "You shall outshine all in attendance."

"Are you and Jane not attending?"

Elizabeth was glad to hear the teasing tone of Mary's voice. "We are, but this dress is truly exquisite."

"He chose it." Mary's cheeks took on a rosy hue. "I was struggling to make a decision about which dresses to order, and Lord Rycroft took the book from me, flipped through it and marked every dress I should choose and told me which colours for a few."

Elizabeth shook her head in disbelief. "A gentleman chose this dress?"

Mary nodded. "And nearly all of my new wardrobe. His taste is superb. Uncle will like him." She hung the dress carefully in her wardrobe. "He even asked Lord Brownlow's sister for a riding habit for me to wear since he guessed we were close in size." She turned to Elizabeth. "He was right. The habit fit as if it had been made for me."

"You must accept him then if he offers," teased Elizabeth. "A man of such talent must not be refused."

Mary giggled but soon grew serious. "He would be a good match for me. I believe I would be happy."

"So you will accept him?"

Mary nodded. "If he offers —."

"He will," interrupted Elizabeth with a smile.

Mary scowled. "If," she emphasized the word, "he offers, I believe I will. It is not too fast, is it? I mean, I have only known him for a very short period of time."

Elizabeth smiled at Mary's look of confusion. It was a familiar look, for she had worn it not long ago before she recognized the feeling that caused it was love. "Who do you think of first in the day? And last before you go to sleep?" Her smile grew as Mary's eyes grew wide. "I shall tell you what Aunt told me. Be brave, my dear sister. Do not let those feelings frighten you, for they will lead to a very happy life for you as they have for me." She gave Mary another hug. "Now, our mother may have need of us. Although I fear if her nerves are not the end of her, they will be the end of me." She opened the door. "It is pleasant being the mistress of your own home instead of the assistant to your mother. It is far less trying to one's nerves."

~*~*~*~*~*~

Mary wrapped her shawl about her shoulders more tightly. She wished to light a fire, but since her reprieve from her mother would only be of a short duration, she chose a blanket for her legs and a shawl for her shoulders. She pulled her feet up under her and leaned her head against the large wing of the chair. A few moments of quiet were what she desired above all before their guests arrived. She knew that few, other than her father, would think of looking in this room for her. It was a small sitting room, tucked away behind her father's study, and, due to its closeness to his sanctuary, it was to remain strictly quiet. Therefore, it was a safe haven for reading and thinking. She allowed her eyes to close, and she drew a deep relaxing breath.

Rycroft pushed the door to the room open slowly and shivered slightly at the coolness of the air. He held high the candle Mr. Bennet had given him as he looked around the room. He saw her in the corner, curled into a ball in a large chair. Her face was peaceful and her shoulders rose and fell as she breathed slowly and steadily. He placed the candle on the table. It must not have been so dark when she first entered, for a candle sat unlit next to her. "Mary," he called softly as he shook her shoulder gently. "Mary."

Her eyes fluttered open for a moment, and she smiled at him before closing them again.

"Mary," he called again. "You must wake."

This time, her eyes snapped open. "Oh," she said as she pulled herself into proper posture. "I did not mean to fall asleep. I only wished a few moments of quiet."

Rycroft chuckled as she immediately checked her hair. "Not a strand out of place," he assured.

"How did you find me?" she asked. "Has everyone arrived? What time is it?"

He stilled her hands and did not let them go but kept them within his. "Your father told me I could find you here. I came early, which I know is poor form, so do not lecture me." He smiled at the scowl she gave him. "It is yet an hour before the others arrive, and an hour and a half before we dine." He rubbed her fingers with his hands. "Your fingers are so cold. I am surprised you do not catch a chill napping in here."

"The rest of me is quite warm," she assured him. "It is only because my fingers were outside of my coverings." She tried to pull her hands out of his. "We should not be here alone," she said softly.

"We have permission from your father," he replied. "Your mother and sisters think I am in your father's study. We are safe." He sat back on his heels where he kneeled beside her chair.

"But someone may come looking for me," she argued.

He shook his head. "Mrs. Darcy will see that they do not."

"And why is that?" asked Mary.

"I have asked her to see to it." He shifted trying to make his position more comfortable.

"You have?"

He nodded.

"So, you have purposed to have a private conversation?" Her heart raced slightly at the thought.

He smiled. "I have." He hoped that the slight widening of her eyes and the faint pink tinge to her cheeks were signs that she would welcome his addresses.

She tipped her head to the side and raised her brow as she smiled at him. "Then, you may wish a chair instead of the floor for comfort."

"Very true." He rose from the floor and pulled

a chair close. "I am not sure how to begin," he said as he sat down. "I wish to marry you, you see, but to just say so seems rather direct and not at all the thing."

Her mouth hung open for a moment before she closed it and gave a small shake of her head. "It is most certainly direct," she said.

"Yes...well..." He tugged nervously at his cravat. "I cannot say I have ever had this conversation with a lady before. I find I am somewhat at a loss." He gave her a wry grin. "Not that I did not spend most of the night and a good portion of the morning thinking of what I should say. However, it seems all my well-thought out words have flown from me." He took her hand. "I knew them until I opened that door and found you sleeping in this chair. You were so charmingly situated, and I thought how privileged I would be to wake with such beauty beside me should you accept me...and they were gone."

Mary felt her cheeks growing very warm, and she ducked her head.

He rubbed his thumb across the back of her hand. "I should have written them down, for I am afraid I am likely to offend you if I speak without preparation."

She giggled. "That bodes ill for marriage if you must always prepare a speech before conversing with your wife."

He laughed. "I had hoped it might come easier with time and practice." He drew a deep breath and gave her a determined look. "Very well, I shall attempt to make my heart known to you without causing offense, if you will promise to stay in this room and tell me if I offend so that I might make my apologies immediately."

"I believe that is a fair arrangement, my lord," she said with a smile.

He shook his head. "I am afraid you must not smile at me, for it will make it far too difficult to make a coherent speech." He placed a finger on her brow. "You must definitely not raise that brow for the expression is far too beguiling." He tipped his head to the side and studied her for a moment. "Perhaps, you should look away."

She shook her head again and laughed. "I have read the papers, my lord, and was under the impression that you were very capable of talking to ladies."

His eyes narrowed. "First, my name is Samuel, not my lord. Second, the ladies you mention, whom I was able to charm to some extent, meant very little to me other than a stolen kiss or a brief moment of pleasure." He looked at his hands which held hers. "It is a life I have left in the past, and a life that was not nearly so debauched as reported."

Mary squeezed his hands. "I am sorry. I should not tease. I had hoped —."

He placed a finger on her lips. "I know, and it did help. Please understand that I do not mind the tease. I just need you to know that the man I was, I am no longer." He paused as if thinking of something. "I would never do as Blackmoore planned. I do not take a wife lightly. She shall not just be the mother of my children and a companion at soirees. She shall be as much a part of me as the air I breathe and the food I eat. She shall be the very beating of my heart, for I have promised myself I would not marry if I were not completely, utterly in love with the lady." He lifted her hands to his lips. "I have found that lady, and she is you, Mary Bennet. Would you do me the great honour of being my wife?"

Mary could not help the tears that slid down her cheeks. How could she accept such love when she had so little to give in return? The thought of it broke her heart. She looked up at the ceiling for a moment before returning her gaze to his.

His heart nearly stopped beating when he saw the sadness in her eyes. He expelled a breath as if he had been hit in the stomach. "You do not want me," he whispered.

Her lip quivered, and she shook her head. "It is not that." She drew in a ragged breath. "How can I accept when my feelings are unequal to such love?" She sniffled.

He drew a breath. "You do not love me?"

"Not as you love me." She lowered her eyes as she could not bear the thought of seeing the pain such an admission was sure to bring.

A small spark of hope sprang into his heart at her confession. "But you love me?"

Her shoulders rose and fell in a sad shrug. "I do not know." She accepted the handkerchief he pressed into her hands and dried her tears. "I had determined I would accept you when I spoke of the possibility with Lizzy, and she assures me that I may indeed love you, but I am unsure. I have…"

She was aware that she was babbling, and so she stopped talking and shrugged once more before adding, "I could not knowingly cause you pain or bear your regret."

"You love me," he said as he drew her to her feet and into his embrace. "You just need time to recognize it." He kissed her gently on the forehead. "I will marry you, Mary Bennet, for my heart demands it." He held her close for another moment before releasing her and moving to the door. "I shall not importune you any further this evening. We shall talk and eat, and no one shall be the wiser. I promise." And with one last look and a bow, he left her drying her eyes and feeling as if part of her very soul had been torn from her body.

Chapter 11

Mary chose a seat near the window where she could work on her stitching. Mrs. Gardiner and her children sat nearby. Mary smiled as she listened to the lilting voice of her aunt, who was reading a story. The Gardiners had arrived only moments before the group from Netherfield had last night. They should have arrived a day earlier, but there had been an issue with an order, and Mr. Gardiner could not leave without attending to it. Mr. Gardiner and her father were tucked cozily in one corner with a deck of cards. Jane sat with her mother going over details for the wedding breakfast while Lydia tried to insert herself into the discussion. Kitty sat next to Mary, a sketch pad on her knees as she drew yet another gown. This one nipped in below the bust as so many did, but it stayed close to the body all the way down to the waist before flaring out.

"I should like to wear that," said Mary peeking over Kitty's shoulder. "You should show it to Mrs. Havelston. She may be able to create it."

Kitty darted a look around the room and then leaned closer to Mary. "I am drawing it for her," she whispered. "You cannot tell a soul, but she liked some of my drawings. She saw them when I was with Jane, and she purchased two." She bit her lip. "I have not yet told Papa. Do you think he will be angry?"

"She bought them?" Mary was surprised by the revelation.

Kitty nodded. "She has promised to keep my name a secret, and I have signed them with only a K for Katherine and an M for Marie. I dared not put my last initial."

Mary agreed that it was wise not to give too many revealing details.

"I know it is not what ladies do," she whispered. "But Mrs. Havelston was so insistent, and uncle seemed to think Papa would not be angry."

"If you are discreet, he may be accepting of the

arrangement," said Mary. "But should it become known…"

Kitty bit her lip and nodded. "I know. It may harm my chances of a good match. I shall be careful." She snapped her book closed as the Netherfield party was announced. She tucked it between the leg of her chair and the wall and took out another that contained drawings of flowers.

Richard crossed the room to take a seat next to Kitty and Mary as he always did on his calls. Mary suspected that it was not only Kitty who enjoyed the other's company. She smiled at Richard as he took his seat and looked toward the door. She blinked. It was empty.

Richard noticed her look of disappointment. "He has gone to London. He was off early this morning, so he should be there by now."

"He left?" She blinked against the tears that sprang to her eyes at the thought.

"Do not fear, Miss Mary. He has promised to return and wished for me to ask you to reserve two dances for him." He pulled a paper from his pocket. "The supper dance and the final dance of the evening." He showed her the paper where those two dances were listed, and then folded it and returned it to his pocket. "He said he had some pressing business to attend and that something which he needed had been left behind in error."

"And this will take three days?"

Richard shook his head. "A bit longer since one of the days is the Lord's Day. That is why he wished to reserve those dances. He was unsure if he would return in time for any of the earlier ones."

Mary nodded and turned back to her stitching. If only her needle could close the hole that had formed in her heart.

"He thought to leave you a note, but with the rumors about the letters, he chose to leave his message with me." He glanced at Kitty and his face turned a slight shade of pink. "There was one more thing."

Mary looked at him expectantly.

"He shall miss you," he swallowed, "and I am to remind you," he blew out a breath, "of his love. He said it in a much more flowery fashion, but I told him I refused to say such things to a lady who was not mine."

Mary bit back a smile as she noted the redness of the colonel's ears. "Thank you. I can imagine that was not an easy message to deliver."

He laughed uneasily. "I would rather lose a boxing match," he mumbled.

"Ah, Miss Mary." Caroline slipped into the chair that was supposed to have been for Rycroft. "I imagine you are excited to return to town and begin your season."

"I am." Mary glanced at Caroline warily. It was not like her to be so friendly. "I am particularly looking forward to returning and seeing Georgiana again."

"Will she not be returning to her brother's house?" Caroline's hand rested dramatically at her heart. To what effect, Mary was uncertain.

"I believe she will, but she is a frequent visitor at Rycroft Place."

Caroline shook her head as if seriously concerned about something. "I cannot understand how your father will allow you to remain living at Lord Rycroft's home after..." She gave a little gasp and leaning close, whispered, "It was not Lord Rycroft who wrote the letter, was it?" She sat back and watched Mary's expression. Seemingly satisfied that she had the right of it, she continued, "To leave his daughter with a man who allowed her to become acquainted with a man who so forward as to write to a lady without an understanding..." She left the thought unfinished and merely shook her head once again. "But, I suppose he is not familiar with how these things go being from the country and all. I am sure he is unaware of Lord Rycroft's reputation?" She looked at Mary with as much contrived concern as Mary guessed could be mustered. "Oh!" her hand flew once again to her heart as dramatically as it had before. "I was thinking how the news of a refusal could add to your interest, but I am afraid it may also come at a great price." She leaned close once again. "Gentlemen like to bet on almost everything, and there is said to be books at their clubs where they place bets on who will become betrothed to whom or who will be," she dropped her voice to a very quiet whisper, "compromised by whom. I should hate to hear it brandished about that your name had been written in such a book."

"I should not like to hear that myself." Mary's hands tightened on the material in her hands. She had not considered what effect news of such a letter might have when she returned to town. She wondered if she would be looked at by the gentlemen as cold or a tease. Neither would be good.

Her discomfort must have been apparent on her face, for Caroline smiled sweetly, if a bit triumphantly, as she added, "I am probably worrying about nothing. Gossip from small towns rarely makes its way into the ton."

"I am sure you are correct." Mary nodded her head but doubted very much that Caroline would keep such a story to herself. She forced her hands to relax their grip on her material and breathed a sigh of relief as Louisa called her sister to her side.

"She is hateful," said Kitty softly. "I should not desire a season if I had to deal with ladies such as her."

"They are not all so unbearable," said Richard dryly. "Some are actually pleasant, but few are very interesting." He sighed. "And I shall soon be expected to select a bride from the lot or accept the one my father selects for me."

"You are not free to choose where you will?" asked Mary.

"Would that I were, but my father controls my inheritance and will do his best to use it to force me into an advantageous marriage."

"That is so sad," said Kitty softly.

He smiled at her. "It is."

"You have no means to stand up to him?" asked Mary.

"I shall be cut off if I do." Bitterness coloured his tone.

"Would you be destitute if that were to happen?" Mary tilted her head to the side and studied his face. Worry creased his brow.

"Not destitute but in need of work and with barely enough to support a wife. Not a meager existence but far lower than I would wish."

"So you would prefer an unhappy existence with plenty?" Mary watched his brows furrow as he considered what she had said. "It would be inconvenient, I suppose, to choose a wife without some means to add to your coffers whether it is to please your father or to ease your life."

He nodded his agreement. "Very inconvenient," he muttered.

"You have your wooden designs," said Kitty. "They are very beautiful. I am confident many would pay to have such items in their homes, so you would not be in need of work."

He smiled. "Very true." His eyebrows raised. "And such work would make me happy."

"A very difficult decision to be sure," said Mary softly.

He nodded again. "Very difficult."

Mary turned her attention back to her stitching and her own troubled thoughts. She longed for someone with whom to share them. She looked at the empty seat beside her. No, she did not long for *someone*; she longed for him.

~*~*~*~*~*~

Mary closed the door quietly and pulled her shawl tight. She sank into her favourite chair and tucked her feet under her skirts.

"A fire would make it more enjoyable."

Mary jumped at the voice. She had forgotten there was an entrance to the room from her father's study. "Papa, you gave me such a fright."

He shuffled over to the bell pull and gave it a tug. "I have been meaning to enjoy this room, and it would not do for me to sit in here in the cold."

He took the chair next to her. The one Rycroft had sat in as he proposed.

Mary swiped at a tear that had escaped her eyes. She had spent more time crying in the past two days than she thought she had in her entire life.

"You miss him?" asked her father, who had not missed the tear.

She bit her lip and nodded.

A servant entered and began to lay the fire. Mr. Bennet began a discussion of the weather and then of the service that morning. When the fire was blazing, and the servant had left, he took Mary's hand. "Speak to me of him. Why did you refuse him?"

She shrugged. "He loves me so much, and I was unsure I could return that love."

Her father patted her hand. "And are you still unsure?"

She shook her head. "No. When he left so suddenly, I felt as though my heart has been ripped in two. And when Miss Bingley began her campaign to unsettle me..."

He nodded, remembering the conversation they had had two days earlier after the Bingleys had left.

"I wished to be able to speak of it to him. I knew in that moment, Papa, that he will always be a part of my heart." She wiped at her eyes again.

"He will return tomorrow, and you may tell him this then." He patted her hand again. "I am so happy that my girls have found such fine gentlemen who will care for them long after I am gone."

"Shhh, Papa," whispered Mary, "do not speak of such things."

"But it is true, my dear. I am not well, and I am old. Those two facts do not bode well for a long life. It is the way of things. Life begins and grows and then fades."

"I know, Papa. All our days are numbered, but I am already enough of a watering pot without considering losing you." She drew a ragged breath. "I love you."

"And I, you, my dear. And I, you." He gave her hand a squeeze. "I have not said it enough." He stood slowly as he heard the door to his study open. "I suspect your uncle is looking for some peace. Do you mind if we join you?"

Mary shook her head. "I would love the company, so long as you do not mind a few tears."

He withdrew his handkerchief from his pocket and placed it on her lap. "I shall send for more if you need them."

She laughed as she picked up the piece of cloth.

"You will tell him tomorrow?"

"Yes, Papa, I will."

"Good. Only two more daughters to go and my duty is done." He reached the adjoining door and called to her uncle to join them. "Have you a handkerchief?" He questioned as her uncle entered the room.

"I do," said Mr. Gardiner.

"Good. Mary may be in need of it." He chuckled. "She is missing a certain gentleman."

"Ah," said her uncle. "I know the feeling well. I can remember the times that my love and I were parted." He settled into a chair and began to tell stories of his courtship.

~*~*~*~*~*~

Rycroft chose a chair near the window where the atmosphere was less boisterous than the rest of the club.

"I hear Blackmoore was unsuccessful with his lady." Endicott took a seat next to Rycroft. "I hear she is all but betrothed to some other gentleman. He followed her to her father's home." He drummed his fingers on the arm of his chair. "The name escapes me," he said.

"Rycroft."

"No, no. I know your name. I cannot remember who it was that hied off after the chit."

Rycroft opened his mouth to reply, but the arrival of Brownlow stopped him.

"I thought you were in Hertfordshire until nearly the new year." He pulled another chair near. "Did she send you on your way?"

"Brownlow, who was it that went after that chit? You know, the one who would not have Blackmoore?" He turned to Rycroft. "He is not happy, I will have you know."

"Endicott," said Brownlow dryly, "neither Rycroft nor I care that he is unhappy."

"Nor do I," said Endicott with a shake of his head. "I was merely relating a fact. Now, do you know the gentleman's name?"

Rycroft shook his head. "I have been in Hertfordshire. Miss Mary is from Hertfordshire." He leaned back in his chair and waited for the connections to be made in Endicott's mind.

"It was Rycroft." Brownlow shook his head. "Honestly, Endicott, you need to keep a notebook with you for recording names."

"Perhaps, I should," he agreed with a shrug. "I suppose I do not need to tell you about it then." He smiled wryly at Rycroft.

"No," said Brownlow as he accepted the cup of

tea the footman had brought for him, "but he must explain why he is here instead of in Hertfordshire."

"True," said Endicott propping his elbows on the arms of his chair and clasped his hands in front of him.

"I came to have the marriage papers drawn up."

"You..." Brownlow's brows rose, and his eyes blinked in surprise. "You offered for her?"

"I did." Rycroft drew a deep breath and released it slowly. "She has not, however, accepted."

Both men looked at him in confusion.

"Then, why are your having papers drawn up?" asked Endicott.

Rycroft motioned to a footman and pointed to the cup of tea Brownlow was holding mid-sip. "Do you remember the details surrounding my cousin's betrothal?"

Brownlow placed both his cup and saucer on the table to his right. "I do."

"Bingley is having a ball," said Rycroft with a smile. "The night before his wedding, Bingley is having a ball, and I shall be in attendance."

Brownlow shook his head as if trying to make sense of it all. "You would compromise her?" he whispered.

"That is our plan." He nodded his thanks to the footman for the tea.

"Our plan?" asked Endicott. "Who is to help you?"

Rycroft allowed the warmth of the tea to settle in his stomach before he responded. "Her father, Bingley, Darcy, the soon-to-be Mrs. Bingley and the delightful Mrs. Darcy." He took another sip of his tea. "I shall return to town a married man. Happily so," he added.

"But, she refused you?" said Endicott, obviously still confused. "How can you be happily married to a lady who does not wish to marry you?"

"Ah," said Rycroft, "but she does. She just has not yet accepted the fact."

Brownlow laughed and shook his head. "I would not be so complacent if I were you. I would fear that she would be angry."

Rycroft sighed. "I am certain I will have to bear a lecture or two, but I am also certain that the price will be worth the payment." He took a long sip of his tea and placed the empty cup on the table. "I love her, and I will not be without her." He held out his hand to shake Brownlow's. "I wish to thank you for sending me off on that errand those many months ago, for it was on my trip back to town when I met her." He rose to leave but thought better of it and sat back down. "My exile, so skillfully arranged by you, gave me time to consider my life." He shrugged. "I did not like what I saw, and so I determined that on my return, I would not be as I had been. I would do my duty to the title and take on the mantle of responsibility I had shirked for so long."

Brownlow smiled. "And happily, your cousin fell into a compromise and had to marry, which brought your path to cross that of Miss Bennet's."

Rycroft nodded. "Precisely. Although, at the risk of sounding the part of a parson, I would say it was providential. Love is a blessing. I hope you both find it." He chuckled as Brownlow rolled his eyes. "I know, my brain has been addled." He rose to leave. "I am in town until the beginning of the week. I would not be adverse to some company or a game of cards once or twice."

"Tomorrow morning. Hyde Park," Brownlow called after him. "Foul weather or clear, we ride."

Rycroft gave him a small salute and then gathered his outerwear and headed toward home.

Chapter 12

Rycroft paced the sitting room. He was to have left for Hertfordshire two hours ago, but thanks to a cat and a cup of tea, his papers were not yet ready.

"Your pacing will not make them arrive any sooner," said his mother peering up from her work.

"I said I would be there before the supper set, and I shall not be." He dropped into a chair. "She will worry."

"It cannot be helped." She turned her eyes back to her work. "The mistress's suite is prepared. I saw to it this morning, and Sarah has moved all of Mary's things into the room." She looked over he glasses at him and smiled. "We are only missing Lady Rycroft." She could not help chuckling at the smile that spread across her son's face at the name.

"Lady Rycroft." Georgiana sighed. "To think she shall not just be my friend but also my cousin."

"And my daughter," said Lady Sophia. "I have waited a long time to have a daughter." She cast a teasing glance at Rycroft. "Although, I had thought it might take longer for the two of you to come to an understanding."

Rycroft's brows rose at the comment.

Lady Sophia chuckled again. "From the moment I met her, I knew she was the one for you, my son. A mother knows these things."

"Indeed?" Rycroft said in disbelief. "And this was the true reason behind your inviting her to stay with us?"

Lady Sophia shook her head. "No, I wished to have her stay with me because I enjoyed her company."

Rycroft, knowing that his mother was relaying only part of the truth with her statement, gave her an amused smile. "Ah. So, it had nothing to do with finding her a husband."

Lady Sophia lifted one shoulder in a nonchalant half-shrug. "The fact that I hoped she would marry my son did make the prospect all that much more enjoyable; although, your wayward tongue did give me a fair bit of concern."

He shook his head and rose to look out the

window once again. "As much as I do not wish to condone such scheming, I find I must thank you for your interference." Seeing his solicitor mounting the steps, he turned and kissed her on the cheek. "I shall bring you back a daughter," he whispered before hurrying from the room as a knock sounded at the door.

Several hours later, Rycroft swung down from his horse and handed the reins to an awaiting groomsman before slipping into Netherfield through the servants' entrance. He stopped long enough in the kitchen to charm a few morsels from the cook and then ascended the back stairs. He paused at the sound of music that filtered through the house to him. Placing the items he carried on the steps and finding the right door, he pushed it open just a crack so that he could peek inside. He had to rise high up onto his toes to see over the ladies standing near the door, but his effort was rewarded as he saw her working her way through the dance. He breathed a sigh of relief as he saw her smiling at something Richard had said. It appeared she was enjoying herself. A footman slipped through the door, and a maid scurried toward him. Rycroft took one last look and saw

Mary looking toward the main entry to the ballroom as she circled away from her partner. He smiled. She was enjoying herself, but not so much that she had forgotten about him. Pleased by the fact, he hurried off to his room. There was not long before the end of the dancing, and he did not wish to attend smelling of horse and the out of doors as he did now.

After a rather cool bath as the water had been waiting for him for some time, he donned his clothes for the ball. As he was standing before the mirror, having his cravat tied, three quick knocks sounded at his door.

"Come," he called.

"It is a relief to see you, Rycroft," said Bingley. "Mr. Bennet is in the library as planned, but I fear you will not have time to meet with him before the final dance." He took a seat.

"He knows of the plan for the dance?"

"He does."

"And he is amenable to it?" Rycroft cast a concerned look over his shoulder toward Bingley.

"He found it quite diverting. I am to stress that it is not proper, but he will not protest. You still have his blessing."

"And Mary? How angry do you expect she will be?" His valet gave a small huff of disapproval, and Rycroft returned to facing the mirror so that his cravat could be given a final straightening.

Bingley shrugged. "I expect she shall be somewhat put out, but according to Jane and Elizabeth, she has been out of sorts and anxious for your return." Bingley chuckled. "I am deliriously happy that Caroline is to leave with Hurst tomorrow, for I expect she will be quite unpleasant."

Rycroft laughed. "It is no more than she deserves."

"Most certainly," agreed Bingley. "She attempted to unsettle Mary the day you left. Richard told me of it."

Rycroft shook his head and clapped Bingley on the shoulder. "For your sake, I pray she finds a husband this season. I still do not know how either you or Darcy tolerate her."

"She is my sister, and Darcy is too bound by propriety to be anything less than a gentleman." Bingley grinned. "Unless, however, she makes a disparaging remark about Mrs. Darcy or her family. You would be right impressed by the glowers and abrupt words he has given Caroline." Bingley opened the door of Rycroft's room. "You should take the servants' stairs. She has not taken her eyes off the door the whole evening."

"Everything is in place?" asked Rycroft as they hurried down the hallway.

Bingley nodded. "The parson is here. The servants are ready to make arrangements for an extra guest. Jane has informed her mother this evening about the wedding breakfast being in honor of both your wedding and mine." He chuckled. "Elizabeth had Mary's things packed after the Bennets arrived here this evening. She is the only one of our group who expects her sister to accept you tonight."

"You truly are agreeable to sharing your wedding day with me?"

Bingley paused in the servant's hall. "Both Jane and I are delighted to be of assistance to you and Mary."

"Thank you." Rycroft tapped his packet of papers on his hand. "Have you seen Miss Mary?" he asked a footman who had just stepped into the hall.

"Yes, sir," he replied. "Two doors down. She is

very near the door." He bowed and continued on his way to attend to his business.

"I shall inform Mr. Bennet of your arrival and the slight change in plans. Wait about five minutes before entering. I shall have him to you before the dancing begins." Bingley did not wait for a reply but trotted down the hall to the door that led to the library.

Rycroft stood outside the door to the ballroom and waited. He paced a few steps forward and back, tapping the papers on his hand as he walked. Finally, he pushed the door open slightly so that he might see her. As his eyes located her, he saw her fan snap shut and her eyes narrow as she turned toward the group of ladies who were whispering near her. A laugh bubbled up inside of him as he prepared to listen to the lecture she was about to give. She would make a formidable countess. He stepped into the room, unable to resist being at her side for a moment longer.

~*~*~*~*~*~

Mary tapped her arm with her fan and watched the door. There were only three dances left, and still he had not arrived. A small twisting began in her stomach and her eyes began to sting as tears gathered in them. Elizabeth nudged her discreetly with her shoulder.

"He will be here," she said.

"But what if something has happened? What if he is hurt? What if he has changed his mind?" She drew a deep breath and expelled it slowly.

Elizabeth slipped an arm around her shoulders. "While an accident is not impossible, it is unlikely. The moon is bright, and I am given to understand he is an excellent horseman. He will be here."

Mary gave her sister a small smile that said she would try to believe what she had been told.

"Miss Mary," said Richard as he bowed upon approaching her, "I believe this is the dance you promised me." He glanced from her worried face to that of Elizabeth's. "That is if you are willing. I would understand if you chose to sit it out."

Mary shook her head and straightened her posture. "I thank you, Colonel, but I believe a dance is just what is needed to keep my mind occupied." She extended her hand to him and allowed him to lead her onto the floor. As she took her place, she noticed her father being escorted from the room. She glanced anxiously at Jane, who was beside her in the line.

"He is tired, and Mr. Bingley has offered him the use of the library," explained Jane. "You know how Mama did not want him to attend."

"Of course," said Mary. "But he is well?"

Jane nodded. "I believe he has found the evening to be very agreeable."

Mary reached over and gave Jane's hand a squeeze. "Thank you. I find I am more anxious than normal tonight."

"I think you are handling things quite well," said Jane as the music began.

As Mary moved through the steps and entered into small conversations with those of her set, her mind did ease, and her eyes looked less frequently toward the door. Soon, she even found herself smiling. If it were not for the dull aching in her heart, she would have found the dance to be thoroughly enjoyable. She curtseyed, thanked Richard and scooted to the side of the room, taking a place where she could easily see the entry. She watched as the next set of couples lined up.

"From a gentleman from town," said a lady to her right in a rather loud whisper. The comment was followed by a tsking.

Mary closed her eyes. It was not the first whisper she had heard tonight. She thought of doing as she had all evening and moving to a new location, but since this offered the best view of the doorway, she remained.

"You know she was in town staying at the home of a gentleman," the lady paused before adding in a scandalized tone, "It was an unmarried gentleman's home. He is an earl to be sure, but you know how titled men can be." She tittered, and the others joined her.

"I hear he arrived a day after the letter," said another. "He met with her father, and two days later, was gone." She gave a small derisive snort. "I have not seen him this evening, so I believe he must have been refused just as the gentleman who wrote to her was." Mary heard a fan snap open. "She'll not see him again. I'd not be so particular if I were her."

Mary, her patience wearing thin, snapped her fan closed. "And why is that?" she asked turning toward the group of gossips. "Would you care to explain why I should not be particular in choosing a gentleman to be my husband? Is it my looks? My intelligence? My family? What exactly is my defect?"

The ladies stood silently, their mouths hanging agape.

"Should I not refuse a man who keeps a mistress and is only looking for a proper wife to bear him children? For the man who wrote me is such a man." She took a step closer to the group of ladies. "Or perhaps I should not take time to carefully consider the offer of a good man because I do not wish to accept unless I can return his affections as ardently as he bestows them?" She crossed her arms and tapped her foot as she waited for a response. Seeing that one was not forthcoming, she sighed. "I would be more particular in my choice of conversational topics if I were you."

"Well said, Miss Mary." Rycroft chuckled. "I was afraid I was the only one to receive such remonstrations — well-deserved remonstrations, I might add." He took her hand and with a sideward glance at the ladies who were watching, lifted it, placing a kiss first on her knuckles and then her palm. A satisfied smile spread across his face as Mary blushed, and the gossips gasped. "I must apologize for being late. There was a mishap with a cup of tea, and my solicitor had to redo a portion of a very important document. I was unable to leave until it was completed." He held up the packet of papers to verify his story both with her and the gossips, who were watching them.

"Ah, Rycroft, at last!" Mary turned to see Mr. Bingley helping her father toward them. "I was awaiting you in the library." He settled into a chair that stood near the wall. "Go, have your fun. We shall talk after."

Rycroft bowed. "Thank you, sir. It is all here as discussed." He handed the packet to Mr. Bennet. "I still have your approval?"

Mr. Bennet's eyes twinkled with merriment as he gave a nod. "It is not a library, but it shall have to do."

Rycroft chuckled. "But it is a ball."

Mr. Bennet winked. "That it is." He made a shooing motion with his hand and then settled in to look at the documents Rycroft had given him.

Rycroft tucked Mary's hand in the crook of his arm, gave a nod of his head to the gossips and led Mary onto the dance floor. "My cousin did deliver my message the day I left?"

"He did." She smiled up at him and said softly, "I have missed you."

"And I, you," he said as they took their places in

line between Jane and Bingley and Darcy and Elizabeth. "It was torturous to know I was going to be late and would cause you to worry."

She smiled at him. "I am just glad you have returned." The first notes of the dance sounded, and she curtseyed to his bow and began the process of working her way through the figures. In sentences broken by the separating and rejoining movements of the dance, he told her of the cat who had upset the tea tray, damaging one page of the document the solicitor had been drafting. She giggled at his recounting. At the end of his story when they once again joined hands, he asked if she wished to know what documents were so important as to have delayed him. She nodded as she circled away from him for a brief moment before rejoining him.

"They are marriage papers," he said as he moved down the center of the line, and instead of releasing her hand and allowing her to circle back to her place, he pulled her into his embrace. "I still intend to marry you, if you will have me." And then, instead of allowing her to reply, he kissed her.

Had she been thinking, she would have been shocked and horrified to be caught in such a scandalously compromising position, but she was not thinking.

"Will you have me?" he whispered when he finally broke away from her.

She nodded and smiled at him. "It seems you have left me no other choice."

He chuckled, but she shook her head when he opened his mouth to speak, and so he remained silent.

She traced the line of his jaw with her finger. "Not because my reputation will be in tatters if I do not, but because my heart will not allow me to refuse. I love you, Samuel Rycroft, and I do not wish to live another moment without you."

He kissed her once more. It was a soft kiss, one that lingered on her lips after he pulled away and left her desiring more. He looked around the room and then back at her. "I brought a special license with me, and I see the parson is here."

Her eyes grew wide. "You wish to marry here? Tonight?"

"I do," he said with a grin. "But, if you prefer, we can wait until tomorrow."

Her brows furrowed. "We cannot marry tomorrow. Jane is getting married tomorrow."

He shrugged. "I do not plan on returning to London without you as my bride." He cocked his head to the side and studied her face, his eyes coming to rest on her lips.

"But such a quick wedding? It just is not done."

"If that were true, Gretna Green would not be the busy place it is." He chuckled as she narrowed her eyes. "Besides, I do believe we have already left the realm of propriety."

She sighed. "Very well. If we are to be completely improper..." She paused and looked at Bingley.

"You are welcome to use my ballroom for your wedding or join us at the church in the morning." He stepped a bit closer and whispered. "You are also welcome to stay here with your husband tonight. Someone can fetch what you need."

She drew a deep breath. "In that case, if the parson is willing, I see no need to delay." She nearly laughed at the look of shock on Rycroft's face. It was quite obviously not the answer he had expected. She cupped his face in her hands. "As I said, I do not wish to live another moment without you, so there really is no other choice." She drew his head down to hers and with a whispered

I love you, pressed her lips against his. If she had been thinking, she would have realized that there were preparations being made around her. If she had been thinking, she might have considered that people were whispering, and Miss Bingley was glowering. But she was not thinking.

She was not thinking of the times he would speak without thought or the moments she would lecture. She was not thinking of the fact that every time this dance played, she would be standing up with him, nor was she thinking of how he would insist on ending each of those dances with a kiss. She was not thinking of the soirees she would attend or the ones she would host. Nor was she thinking of his mother, who was anxiously awaiting a daughter, or the friend who was awaiting a new cousin. She was not thinking of the family that would grow around and within her starting this very night. No, Mary Bennet was not thinking. She was only kissing and loving and embracing what was surely to become her greatest source of happiness. For when one's heart swells as hers had when she had seen him standing behind her, when one's lips have tasted such sweet and consuming love, and when one's mind knows that despite the trials that might come, it will not be at rest without the man whose lips are pressed against hers and whose arms surround her, there really is no other choice.

Acknowledgements

There are many who have had a part in the creation of this story. Some have read and commented on it. Some have proofread for grammatical errors and plot holes. Others have not even read the story (and a few, I know, will never read it), but their encouragement and belief in my ability, as well as their patience when I became cranky or when supper was late or the groceries ran low, was invaluable.

And so, I would like to say *thank you* to Zoe, Rose, Betty, Kristine, Ben, and Kyle, as well as my faithful readers on my blog and at darcyandlizzy.com.

I have not listed my dear husband in that group because to me he deserves his own special thank you, for without his somewhat pushy insistence just over a year ago that I begin sharing my writing, none of my writing goals and dreams would have been met.

Choices Book Three:
His Inconvenient Choice

Coming to your favourite e-tailer late winter 2016

FROM CHAPTER 1

January 1, 1812

Colonel Richard Fitzwilliam unfolded the small piece of paper that had been tucked into his pocket as he left Netherfield after the wedding breakfast. He shook his head. Two cousins and a friend married all within the space of two weeks was enough to set anyone's world on end. It was also the sort of thing that made him contemplate his own future. Such thoughts often made his breathing feel forced. He drew a deep breath, trying to rid his body of the feeling of being crushed, but it was only slightly helpful. He knew that his future was not to be as happy as those of his cousins and Bingley. He was not free to choose where he wished. His marriage would be one of convenience; his father would see to that.

He looked surreptitiously at the paper in his palm, not wishing to draw attention to it from the others in the carriage. The drawing there brought a smile to his lips and a pang of regret to his heart. Forget-me-nots graced the lid of a box from which spilled strands of pearls and chains of gold. He folded the drawing again and slipped it back into his pocket. If his heart could make his choice for him instead of his father, Kitty Bennet would be his choice. She had stolen his heart when she shivered in the wind on the street in front of the milliner's shop as she insisted on being introduced to him as Katherine. Upon further acquaintance, she had proven to be a lady who shared many of his same interests and who made him feel at ease. She expected no more from him than to be himself. He did not need to be a military leader or the son of an earl. She was interested in his wooden creations — and not as a lady who was trying to make a favourable impression on a gentleman. No, she listened with interest and animation. She had even sketched a few designs that he might like to use.

"If you could wait but a year," she had said as they strolled the perimeter of the ballroom last evening, "then your inheritance would be yours."

"He will not allow me to be free. He will insist on my marrying before he gives me one farthing more than I have," he had replied. Her eyes had filled with tears that she refused to shed, and his heart had broken a bit more at the thought of a life without her. "If I could wait," he had whispered. "I would wait a thousand years for you."

She had smiled sadly at him and said, "And I would wait for you."

He ran his gloved finger over the drawing in the pocket of his coat. "Do not forget me," she had said as she had slipped the drawing into his pocket when he was taking his leave of her. He knew he would never forget her. His hand closed around the paper.

"You are looking rather pensive, Colonel," said Caroline Bingley. "Are they pleasant thoughts?"

"Not all of them," he said as he turned to look out the window. If the weather had not been so foul, he would have refused Hurst's offer to travel with him.

"That is a pity," said Louisa. "I prefer to think on pleasant things whenever possible."

"As do I," said Richard, "but it is not always possible."

"A colonel must have many unpleasant things to consider," added Caroline.

"He must," said Richard. "However, I was not thinking as a colonel but as a mere man."

Hurst snorted at the comment. "Do leave him be, Caroline."

"I was only attempting to pass the time in conversation," she replied with a huff. "The light is too poor for anything else."

"I find a quiet nap a most refreshing way to pass a trip," replied Hurst.

"How dull," said Caroline.

"Not at all," said Richard. "I find I would like to close my eyes. It has been a busy two days."

Hurst nodded. "You were out with your men yesterday, were you not?"

"I put them through a few drills to test them.

Those who passed were allowed to attend the ball. Those who did not pass were confined to quarters for the evening." It had been his plan, and a successful one, to keep Wickham from the ball. He would take every opportunity afforded him by his position to ensure that Wickham had less pleasure than he desired. It was the one pleasure he received from his duty.

"And, I believe, you danced every dance, did you not?" asked Louisa.

"All save one." His heart pinched, for that one had been set aside to stroll with Kitty.

"Oh, Hurst, you are right. I do believe a nap must be had. What with an early morning yesterday for the colonel, a night of dancing, and another early start to the day today, he must be very tired." She turned to Caroline. "It would be unkind of us to keep him from his rest."

"I thank you," said Richard with a bow of his head. Then added, "I am indeed rather tired," as he settled back and closed his eyes.

Conversation with anyone at present would be unpleasant; with Caroline Bingley, it would be even more so. His fingers once again sought that slip of paper in his pocket. Finding it, he allowed his mind to wander to the lady who had given it to him, and with a deep exhale, he attempted to find some peace in sleep.

~*~*~*~*~*~

"Mr. Darcy, might I have a word with you?" Kitty turned from the window where she had been watching the Hursts' carriage drive away. There were not many wedding guests remaining, and she knew that both she and the Darcy's would leave soon.

"Certainly," replied Darcy. He had not had very many opportunities to speak with Kitty. She seemed to avoid him whenever possible, and so her request surprised him. He watched her twist her fingers together and bite her lip, signs that he had learned through watching his wife indicated she was nervous.

"I have a little bit of money and expect to receive some more." She resisted the urge to duck her head and hide from him. His presence had always unsettled her. She was sure he was at any moment going to scold her for some foolishness. She knew she had no reason to feel so, but she did. However, she also knew that he would best be able to advise her, and so she straightened her shoulders and continued. "I have sold some designs to Mrs. Havelston, and she has requested some more. I have not signed them with my name, and it is to be a secret arrangement." The words rushed from her. "I would like to invest it. I know that you can earn money with money, but I do not know how to do it, and I am not a gentleman, which limits me."

He smiled at her. "That sounds like a wise thing to do."

Her brows drew together. "It does?"

"Indeed." He smiled at her and was rewarded with a small smile in return.

She withdrew a small velvet pouch from her reticule. "It is really very little. It may not be enough to invest yet, but I dare not place it in my father's strongbox, for if something happens to him, I do not wish to explain it to Mr. Collins."

Darcy took the bag from her and slipped it into his pocket. "I shall care for it. You will keep a record of what you have given me, and I will do the same. You know how to do this?"

She pursed her lips and drew her brows together. "I will have my father show me."

"Very good."

"Mr. Darcy, could we save some time and trouble if I request my uncle to give the money to you?" She twisted her hands again. "He receives payments from Mrs. Havelston for her orders, so no one would suspect she is paying me if she gives it to him. And if he meets with you, no one would question the activity."

He nodded. The thought she had put into her plans impressed him. If he were perfectly honest with himself, he would not have thought her capable of such well-thought out plans. She had on the occasions before his marriage to Elizabeth struck him as flighty and silly. He chided himself. He had not noted such behaviour since their arrival last week. "I understand. This is an arrangement that is to be private."

"Very. If anyone was to learn that I was earning money..."

"I understand," said Darcy. "Do you have a plan in mind for the money?"

The tears that had been threatening all morning sprang to her eyes, and her cheeks flushed in embarrassment.

"You do not have to tell me," Darcy said quietly.

She shook her head. "I have a foolish notion that will probably be unsuccessful, but your cousin should not be forced to give up what he loves. I thought perhaps I could help him find a way to be happy." She shrugged. "If not, then the money can be added to my portion, which will be of assistance to me when I need to set up my own establishment. I do not wish to live solely on the charity of my relations."

"You do not plan to marry?" Darcy asked in some surprise.

The tears once again gathered in her eyes, and she blinked against them as she shook her head. "I had hoped," she said softly.

His eyes followed her gaze toward the window and the drive at Netherfield. "One must not lose hope, Miss Kitty. Circumstances can change."

She drew a deep breath and released it slowly as she steadied her emotions. Then, she gave him as much of smile as she could manage. "While I own that it is not an utter impossibility, I think it highly unlikely."

He nodded as she thanked him and went to join her father who was saying his farewells to Elizabeth and Jane. Elizabeth caught his eye and gave him a questioning look and in response he shrugged and smiled.

"You look troubled, my dear," she said as she slipped her arm into his and waved to her father's carriage.

"I believe I am," he said as he assisted her into their carriage. Then, he gave one more wave to Bingley and climbed in beside her. He shook the rain from his hat and set it on the bench across from them before tucking a blanket across their laps. "Shall we pass the journey as we did on our wedding day?"

She giggled. "I should like that very much, Mr. Darcy, but not until you tell me what has you troubled. I shall not be distracted by your sweet kisses until I know all."

"Is that a fact?" He leaned over and kissed her softly.

She smiled and pushed at his chest. "I would like nothing better than to be distracted so pleasantly, sir, but I am afraid my mind will not be settled until you have told me about what you and Kitty were speaking."

He gave her a quick kiss before she could stop him. "Very well. Your sister has asked me to help her with her finances. It seems she has sold some designs and intends to sell some more, and she wishes to have her earnings invested."

"And this has you troubled?" Elizabeth's brows furrowed as one eyebrow rose in disbelief. "Is it that she is earning money which has concerned you?"

He chuckled and shook his head. "Her selling designs and wishing to invest is not what has me troubled. I asked her what she intended to do with the money, and she nearly cried." He stroked Elizabeth's cheek with his thumb and smiled sadly at her. "Based on her answers and my cousin's strange behaviour last night and this morning, I believe she has had her heart broken by my uncle." He first gave her pursed lips a kiss and then the deep furrow between her brows. "She wishes to help Richard with her money. She does not wish to see him forced to give up what he loves. She also said she no longer intends to marry." He wrapped his arms around Elizabeth and drew her closer as he saw the sadness enter her eyes. "And that has me troubled, for I do not wish to see either her or Richard give up who they love."

"What can be done?" Elizabeth peeked up at him from where her head rested on his shoulder.

"I do not know. My uncle will make it challenging. He wishes a marriage of advantage for Richard, one that will strengthen his political ties and increase Richard's wealth. It will take some thought. However, nothing can be done at present." He kissed her forehead again. "And now, Mrs. Darcy, since I have told you all that is troubling me, I believe I may now distract you with kisses."

She wrapped her arms around his neck. "I believe you must." And eagerly, he obliged.

Choices Book One:
Her Father's Choice

FROM CHAPTER 1

NOVEMBER 26, 1811

The music swirled about Elizabeth as she completed the final few steps of the dance. As the last notes of the song faded into the expanse of Netherfield's ballroom, she dipped a curtsey and moved silently away from her dancing partner. The swirling feeling, however, did not die with the music. From the corner of her eye, she could see Miss Bingley moving toward her. Speaking to anyone, let alone Miss Bingley, was not something she wished to do at present, so seeing an opportunity to slip away from the crowds, she took it. She smiled at her father as she slid behind him and out of the room into the hallway. Assuring herself that no others would see her escape, she hurried to the library. A need for solitude, somewhere to gather her thoughts and sort through the strange feelings that had her nerves all aflutter, consumed her. She clicked the door quietly shut behind her and retrieved a book of poetry from the shelf. It was one of the books she had enjoyed reading when she had stayed here to tend to her sister.

Darcy watched her slip off her shoes and tuck her small feet under her skirts as she curled into the chair and flipped the pages of her book. His book lay open on his lap, but not one word had entered his mind for it was filled with the lady who now presented such a charming picture before him. *This*, he thought to himself, *this is how an evening at home should be spent.* The thought both shocked and pleased him. He shook his head and smiled, for he could not help it even in his unsettled state of mind. Thoughts of Miss Elizabeth often led him to smile. He allowed himself several moments to consider her, to play again in his mind many of their interactions before he turned his mind to his book.

As fair as thou, my bonnie lass,

So deep in luve *am I;*
And I will love thee still, my dear,
Till a' the seas gang dry.[1]

Darcy closed the book. *So deep in love am I*, the words of Mr.Burn's poem, repeated themselves in his mind. That must be it. His disquiet, his agitation of spirit, the joy of having her near and the torment of hearing her speak of another were not symptoms that his heart might be in danger of being engaged but rather signs that it was already engaged and, he feared, to an unalterable extent. Quietly, he lay the book on the table next to his chair and rose to leave. He would return later to retrieve the book so that he might ponder the words and what he was to do about his heart.

Elizabeth glanced up at Darcy as he walked to the door and flipped yet another unread page. The book had not been able to capture her mind or quiet her spirit. The room still spun slowly, her heart still fluttered, and her eyes were drawn of

---

1. Burns, Robert, and Anonymous. "A DAY WITH THE POET BURNS." *The Project Gutenberg EBook of A Day with the Poet Burns by Anonymous. Project Gutenberg, 15 Feb. 2011. Web. Poem quoted is "My Luve is Like a Red, Red Rose." Book originally published by Hodder and Stoughton, London.*

their own accord to the man sitting across the room from her. Perhaps once he took his leave of the room, she might find the peace she sought. She turned her mind back to her book; but it was of no use, the desire to read seemed to be leaving with Mr. Darcy. So she stood, smoothed her skirts and slipped her feet into her slippers.

The door opened as Darcy reached it, and Elizabeth's aunt, Mrs. Phillips, entered. She looked from Mr. Darcy to Elizabeth, who was still smoothing her skirts, and then peered around the room as if searching for someone or something. Her eyes grew wide and her hand flew to her chest. "Oh," she said. "Oh, my. Oh, Lizzy. And…and Mr. Darcy." She spun on her heels and very nearly ran from the room. "Mr. Bennet," she called. "Mr. Bennet, you are needed."

Elizabeth gasped. "I must stop her, " she said as she moved toward the door, but Darcy stopped her.

"The damage has already been done, " he said. "Should you follow after her, she will only make a greater spectacle as she either scolds or questions you. It is best to await your father here." He led her back to her chair. Reluctantly, he let go of her arm as she took a seat. "Are you well?" he asked.

"I hardly know," she replied. Thoughts of the things her aunt might be saying filled her mind. She sought a solution, an explanation that might explain her current circumstances in such a way as to repair her reputation. She watched Mr. Darcy pace about the room and replied to his inquiries after her health. He sat for a moment but stood again and resumed his pacing, which only stopped when her father entered. Then she noted how very rigid his stance became.

"Papa," she said rising and going to him, "it is not how my aunt presented it." Her father pulled her into his embrace.

"It is not about what has happened, my Lizzy, but about what others think has happened," he said quietly. "I do not doubt your honour, but you know how the gossips work." He released her from his arms and grasping her chin, forced her to look at him. The pain in her eyes was nearly his undoing. "Have a seat while we discuss what might be done to save your reputation," he faltered for a moment before adding what he knew would play most heavily upon her heart, "and the reputation of our family." He clenched his jaw as he saw her eyes grow wide and fill with tears.

"There is only one option, sir," said Mr. Darcy. "I must marry your daughter. My reputation may be tainted slightly by a situation such as this, but the damage that would be done to Miss Elizabeth...." He silently reproved himself once again for not having left the room when she entered.

"I believe you have the right of it, Mr. Darcy. There seem to be few other options. I know my wife's sister is not one to keep a story such as this to herself. I fear the entirety of Mr. Bingley's guests have already come to know of it."

Panic gripped Elizabeth's heart. Surely, her father could not be serious. Marry Mr. Darcy? She shook her head. "No, Papa, please," she begged. She blinked against the tears that threatened to fall.

"Elizabeth, there is no other option. You will marry Mr. Darcy." His voice was gentle but firm, and she knew from his use of her full name instead of Lizzy that there was no hope of changing his mind.

"No," she said softly as she buried her face in her hands and allowed the tears to fall.

She felt his arm come around her shoulders. "My dear daughter, it is for the best. Aunt Phillips is not known for her discretion, and the story of your being alone in the library with Mr. Darcy will be circulated, and embellishments will be added. Your betrothal is all that will save your reputation. We must also think of your sisters."

Her shoulders shook as she sobbed quietly, but she nodded her head as if she understood the reality of the situation.

Mr. Bennet swallowed the lump in his throat and strengthened his resolve. This was for the best, even if his heart broke at seeing her so unhappy. "It will be a good thing, Lizzy. I know you do not see it now, but I truly believe there is no one better suited to you than Mr. Darcy." He kissed the top of her head. "Dry your eyes." He gave her hand a squeeze as he stood to address Mr. Darcy. "I do not question your honour. I am convinced this is nothing more than an unfortunate chain of events, but the gossip will not present it as such." His conscience pricked him as he said it. Truly, it was not Darcy's honour he questioned as much as his own.

"How shall we proceed?" Darcy's voice was tight.

"It might be best if we give everyone time to adjust to the sudden circumstances," suggested Sir

William. "A meeting could be arranged for tomorrow."

Darcy nodded mutely, perhaps a few hours to accept their new relationship was what both he and Miss Elizabeth needed. He had been pleased to watch Elizabeth resting in the library. He had imagined her reading at Pemberley, an idea which had taken him by surprise. He had known he was somewhat in danger of having his heart engaged, but he had not expected it to happen so suddenly and without a greater amount of warning. There had been no unease at the thought. It had been as natural as wishing to see his sister, Georgiana. And now as he watched Elizabeth weep at the idea of marrying him, his heart ached.

"Might I have a few moments with Miss Elizabeth before she leaves?" He was not sure what he could say to ease her distress, but he felt an overwhelming need to at least attempt some sort of comfort.

Mr. Bennet gave him a sympathetic smile and nodded his consent. The request, coupled with the look of concern on Darcy's face, eased his mind a bit. His daughter would be loved. Indeed, it appeared she already was. If only she could see past her first impression of the gentleman....

Mr. Bennet had attempted to paint Darcy in a favourable light, but no matter how hard he had tried, Elizabeth had clung to her opinion that Darcy was proud and disdained everything about her, her family, and the neighbourhood. She was wrong, of course. He had done some shooting with Darcy and Bingley and had found both gentlemen to be pleasant; although, Darcy was more reserved and thoughtful. He pulled the door closed as he and Sir William entered the hall.

"We have done what is best, have we not?" Mr. Bennet looked to his friend for reassurance.

Sir William shrugged. "Whether it is best or not, it is done. We must trust that they will eventually be happy together." He leaned against the door frame across from Mr. Bennet. "Consider the facts. Collins was set to make an offer which would have led to a great upheaval in your household when Elizabeth refused him — for you know she would." Mr. Bennet nodded his agreement. Elizabeth had made her dislike for the gentleman perfectly clear to everyone save to her mother and Mr. Collins.

Sir William continued, "Then, there were Miss

Bingley's comments about quitting the neighbourhood. That will not happen so quickly now, which will give Jane a greater chance of being happily matched. After all, news of one wedding often leads to news of others. And," he held up his finger to highlight the point, "it would be desirable to Bingley to be closely related to Darcy. His standing would increase and the felicity between their wives would serve both men well." He shifted and crossed one leg over the other. "There is also the fact that Mr. Wickham has been showing particular attention to Elizabeth, and from rumors I have heard, he is not the sort of man a father wishes to have pay court to his daughter." He sighed. "There are no guarantees, but I do believe your choice will prove to be best…in time."

Mr. Bennet leaned his head back and closed his eyes. He prayed that he had made the right choice and that, one day, his daughter and his new son would forgive him for his interference.

A Leenie Brown Sampler

A selection of short samples from Leenie's other books

OXFORD COTTAGE

It had been a frustrating day. Fitzwilliam Darcy and Charles Bingley had set out from London just as the sun was creeping its way above the horizon. They had ridden hard ahead of the carriages that were bound for Netherfield. The servants would see to the unloading of their things as they paid a visit to the office of Bingley's solicitor, Mr. Phillips.

Darcy had been impressed with the knowledge and efficiency of Mr. Phillips; it was no wonder his uncle had recommended the man. Now, after following that man's directions, which had them wandering in what seemed like circles in a woods somewhere in Hertfordshire, they had been directed by a kindly gentleman to seek shelter from the coming deluge at a cottage located somewhere in that same woods.

The spitting rain had left muddy trails down Darcy's great coat as it mixed with the road dirt. Keeping to the right branch of the road as the gentleman had instructed, Darcy found himself riding up a path toward a stone cottage. "I think this is the cottage," said Darcy.

"I do not see any other," agreed Bingley.

Darcy saw a young woman sitting beneath a structure made for storing firewood. Her bonnet hung down her back. She brushed a stray strand of hair the color of fine chocolate from her face with a gloved hand. Then she returned to the task of removing soil from her gardening tools. Darcy and Bingley dismounted and walked toward her.

~*~*~*~*~

Elizabeth was intent on getting the dirt removed from her tools before storing them. Her father had given her a challenge, and she was determined not to fail. She batted at a curl that had, as was its wont, worked its way free of her pins and fallen into her face.

The soft, dripping and dropping of the rain on the roof of the wood stand was relaxing. She was glad that she had gotten the last of the seedlings transferred to the flower garden—tucked under their protective blanket of straw before the rain began. She worked as quickly as she could, wishing to be inside the cottage before the rain started in earnest. She knew that the roof over her head and the wall that faced the prevailing winds would keep her dry while she worked, but she did not relish the thought of rushing through a downpour to reach the house. She would just bide her time in the wood stand if it were not for the fact that Jane and Mary were expecting her to help with dinner preparations. So deep in thought and so concentrated on the task at hand was she that she jumped when she heard his voice.

~*~*~*~*~*~

"Good day," called Darcy as he and Bingley approached her. The young woman jumped to her feet in surprise, a rake clattering to the ground. He halted a distance from her and said gently, "My apologies. I did not mean to startle you, ma'am. We were told that we might find refuge from the rain at Oxford Cottage." He swept a hand toward the house. "Is this Oxford Cottage?"

Elizabeth smiled. There was only one person who could have sent these men to her cottage. "Indeed it is, sir. My sisters and I would be happy to provide shelter for you until the rain passes." She retrieved the fallen rake and tucked it, along with her other tools, behind the wood pile against the structure's one wall.

"Your horses may take refuge here." She indicated a rail where the horses could be tied; then, walking to the far end of the woodpile, she retrieved a pail of rain water.

Darcy watched her offer the pail of water to each of the horses, stroking their necks and cooing to them softly. She was captivating; there was no way around the fact. His heart had lurched, actually lurched, inside his chest when she had smiled at him. Now, witnessing her tender care of his horse—his prize possession, the stallion that he had raised and trained from a colt—he was well and truly lost.

"Allow me," he said as he took the pail from her

and carried it back outside the structure to collect more water.

Her fingers brushed his briefly as she allowed him to take the pail from her. She shook and stretched her hand as she tried to stop the sudden tingling sensation that coursed through her fingers and up her arm.

"If we wish to enter the cottage before the torrents begin, we need to hurry." Snatching up the hem of her skirt slightly to avoid some of the mud, she walked quickly toward the cottage. Had she been alone, she would have raced, but since she was in the company of two gentlemen—two handsome gentlemen—she tried to maintain some modicum of propriety.

Elizabeth called to her sisters as she took the gentlemen's coats and hats and placed them near the fireplace in the sitting room. The rain had not been heavy, but their outerwear was damp and needed drying. Besides, it gave her an opportunity to study the gentlemen surreptitiously.

There was something familiar about the man who had startled her. She felt as if she had seen him before. He was beautiful—tall with broad shoulders, dark hair that hung down around his ears and across his forehead, a face that was not youthful and yet not aged either, and his eyes, they were a piercing blue. Elizabeth was quite sure that she could spend many contented hours studying those eyes, as well as most everything else about him. Feeling a faint blush beginning to creep its way up her neck and towards her cheek, she turned her eyes away from him and examined his friend.

The second gentleman was quite fine to look upon as well—slightly shorter and narrower of frame with golden hair that curled about in a rather haphazard array. He wore the expression of an exuberant youth although his face was not much younger in appearance than that of his friend. Her examination of this gentleman was interrupted by the entrance of Jane and Mary, although in reality, her attention had not been fully focused on him at all as her eyes had wandered more than once back to his much more temptingly handsome friend.

Darcy watched the two young ladies enter the room. One was fair and classically handsome. The other was dark like the sister he had met by the woodpile but wore a more serious mien. He wondered to himself how one small cottage could contain such an abundance of beauty.

FOR PEACE OF MIND

Mr. Gardiner gave a small snort and shifted in his seat. Elizabeth glanced at her dozing uncle. She was glad to be in his carriage and moving away from Longbourn.

She tried to read the book that had lain open to the same page for the last half hour, but it was no use. Her mind would not stop repeating the events of the last few days. She sighed and looked out the window.

She had tried to avoid Mr. Collins, and aside from one dance at the Netherfield ball and those horrible few moments spent together a day ago, she had been successful. But it was those few moments confined in the breakfast room that had done the damage. Her cousin had managed to announce his intentions and had not been willing to accept her refusal. A great stir had arisen in the wake of her rejection, and now her mother steadfastly ignored her, save to complain loudly about her whenever she was near.

Her father had only tolerated the disturbance for a few hours before sending an express to request Mr. Gardiner's advanced arrival in Meryton and his willingness to return home with not just Jane but also Elizabeth. And so, Elizabeth Bennet sat in the carriage next to her sister. She had been sent away—sent away for her own good and her father's peace of mind.

Elizabeth closed her book and tucked it into her reticule. She studied her sister for a moment. Jane dabbed at her eyes, and Elizabeth gave her hand a small squeeze.

Jane smiled at her, but the smile did not reach her eyes. "I shall be well. A little time is all that is needed to get over a disappointment, or so I have been told."

"We have also been told to keep an eye out for husbands." Elizabeth spoke softly so as not to disturb her uncle. "I dare say if I do not return home with a prospect, Mama shall disown me and throw me into the hedgerows."

"She really was quite put out with you, was she not?" Jane could not help the small chuckle that escaped her.

"Was?" Elizabeth huffed. "She still is."

Mr. Gardiner shifted again in his seat as the carriage began its halting journey through the streets of London. He yawned and stretched. "Your cousins will be glad to see you. Andrew has been planning a trip to the park with you, Lizzy. Margaret would like to have Jane help her with a bonnet. Michael has several stories already chosen for reading, and Amelia helped Cook make some special cakes for your arrival." He peered out the window. Elizabeth loved how anxious he was to be home. She wished that she could one day feel the same about her home.

Finally, the carriage rattled to a stop before the Gardiners' townhouse. A smile spread across Mr. Gardiner's face. "There, did I not tell you they would be eager to see you?"

Andrew was first to exit the house, followed by Mrs. Gardiner and her three other children. The children shifted and danced behind their mother, eagerly waiting to greet their cousins.

"My dears, it is so good to see you." Mrs. Gardiner gave each girl a warm embrace as she alighted from the carriage. "As soon as the children have given you a proper welcome, we will have tea and cakes in the drawing room."

Three-year-old Michael bounced up and down. "Cake, cake, cake," he said, grabbing Elizabeth's hand and pulling. "Mia make cake."

"So your father said," Elizabeth replied as she allowed herself to be pulled into the house.

The Gardeners did not live in a very fashionable section of town. Their house was modest but well-kept and comfortable. Uncle Gardiner ran a prosperous import and export business not far from his home, and although he could afford to live in a more upscale district, he preferred to stay close to his business and the friends that lived in the community. They employed several servants, and their children had a nurse and a governess. But, to the outside world, their address left them out of many circles.

Within these walls, a familial warmth radiated to everyone who entered as if the home had some magic to soothe even the weariest of individuals. But Elizabeth knew that it was not the building that held the magic, but the family within it. She watched as Amelia proudly and properly served her cakes, and Margaret poured tea under the supervision and instruction of her mother. She smiled with contentment.

After the children had had their treats and the attention of their favourite cousins for some time, they returned to the nursery, and Jane and Elizabeth were allowed to settle in and refresh before dinner. Elizabeth lay on the bed, looking at the ceiling.

"It is nice to be here, is it not? I so love Aunt and Uncle and their children."

"As do I," said Jane as she joined her sister on the bed.

"If I ever get married and have a family, I would wish for a home like this. Full of love and welcoming."

Jane nodded her agreement. "I love Mama and Papa with all my heart, but theirs is not a marriage I wish to copy."

"Nor I," agreed Elizabeth. "I will only marry someone whom I love and respect and who is my equal in intellect." Elizabeth sat up, "And, he cannot be the sort of man who does not encourage his wife to learn and read. I fear marriage for me is an impossibility!" She flopped back on the bed. "I am sure such a man does not exist! Instead, I will have to be satisfied to live with you and your family and care for your children. I will teach them to read and write and question everything they hear."

Jane grabbed a pillow and threw it at her. "I do not for one moment believe that you will be a spinster." She lay down on the bed next to Elizabeth. "But, I should love to have you live with me always."

Elizabeth rolled over and propped herself up onto her elbows to look at Jane. "And because I love you, I will promise to teach your children some decorum, so that they are not as silly as our younger sisters. I love Papa dearly, but I will never be diverted by my children's improprieties. I fear it is our family's unseemly behaviour that has brought you so much sorrow, my dear sister." She scowled. "I am sure that arrogant man persuaded Mr. Bingley to leave because your connections were below him."

"Elizabeth," Jane chided. "You cannot go around making assumptions about the actions of others. You are far too hard on Mr. Darcy. If anyone is to blame, it is Mr. Bingley's horrid sister."

"Why, Jane," said Elizabeth proudly, "I do believe that is the most unkind thing you have ever said."

Jane smiled in response. "We should go to Aunt. I am sure she is waiting for us."

Downstairs, the Gardiners sat quietly talking in the drawing room as they waited for their nieces to join them for dinner. Jane and Elizabeth were favourites of the Gardiners and their children. Both girls were well-mannered and caring. Although Elizabeth could at times let her tongue and temper get the better of her, she was usually quick to right the wrong and worked diligently to keep herself under good regulation. Jane was sweet to a fault. Steady and easy-going, she was quick to find the good in all and in all situations. The two girls balanced each other perfectly. Elizabeth challenged Jane to take risks while Jane calmed Elizabeth and helped to soothe her when she became irritated.

"Do you know any gentlemen to whom we might introduce our nieces while they are in town?"

Mr. Gardiner scrunched up his face and rubbed his chin while he thought. "There is my former partner's son. He is to come to dinner tomorrow. I should think he would do quite well with Jane, and perhaps he has a strong-minded friend he might be willing to introduce to our Lizzy." He laughed softly. "It would have to be a very strong-minded young man. Matlock's nephew comes to mind, but

I am not sure Matlock would wish a connection to trade."

"My dear, I may be partial, but any gentleman with good sense and an eye for prosperity should beg for a connection to you."

Mr. Gardiner patted his wife's hand. "I quite like your partiality, my love." He stood and offered his arm to her as his nieces entered the drawing room, followed by his three eldest children. "I believe dinner awaits."

TEATIME TALES

From A Music Room Meeting

A melody, haunting and beautiful, drew Harriet down the hall. Quietly, she opened the door and slipped silently into the room, taking a seat directly behind the player.

His body moved with the emotion of the music, falling forward, raising back, following his hands as they moved up or down the instrument. The melody seemed to flow from him as if it were a part of him being breathed into existence. She dashed away a tear. How was it that a man such as he could make the air swirl with emotion. She had not even known he played. The gentleman before her clashed with the person she had always known. He was the one everyone looked to for strength. He was the one to lighten the mood with a well-placed, though not always proper, joke. Unless severely provoked, he was always a picture of cheerful composure.

His fingers held the last chord until it faded into silence. Only then did his hands fall away from the keys. His shoulders sagged, and his head drooped for a moment before he straightened, assuming his normal rigid pose.

She paused for a moment to admire his form before alerting him to her presence. "I did not know you played, Colonel."

Richard spun around. "Miss Phillips!" He stood quickly and bowed. "I did not hear you enter."

She smiled at him. "As intended." She raised an eyebrow at him. "I was afraid you would stop playing if you knew I was here." She motioned for him to take a seat next to her.

He chuckled. "I would have."

"You play very well."

"Thank you. It is my mother's doing. She

insisted on all her children learning at least one instrument."

"At least one instrument? Do you play anything else?"

He inclined his head in acknowledgement. "I do."

"Which?" She leaned toward him in anticipation.

He shook his head. "One disclosure is enough for tonight. The others shall remain my secret. " His eyes searched the room. "Perhaps you could share a secret with me since you have discovered one of mine. How is it that you are here unattended? Surely you did not arrive at tonight's fete unaccompanied. Lillesley would never hear of such a thing. He did escort you, did he not?" Her brothers had always taken prodigious care of their sisters, especially Harriet as she was the youngest and most prone to finding trouble.

"He did, but he was quite preoccupied with several debutantes and their mothers. It seems unusually easy for some ladies to shift their preference from one gentleman to another. I suppose it is the title they truly admire." There was a hint of bitterness in her words.

"Forgive me. I have not had the opportunity to extend my condolences to you on the passing of your brother."

"Thank you, but it has been nearly a year." She smiled sadly. "Yet it seems so much longer. Edmund has struggled to find his feet with all the new responsibilities that have fallen to him. Has he written to you about it?" Colonel Edmund Phillips, now Lord Lillesley, had been on the continent with Richard when the news of his brother Matthew's death had summoned him home.

Richard shrugged. "He has made mention of some of his difficulties, but I believe he looks more to my brother and father for guidance on such matters than myself. What do I know about the business of being a viscount and sitting in the House of Lords?" Since childhood Richard and Edmund had scampered along behind their brothers, following their footsteps but knowing they were the lesser sons. There had been a comfort in the understanding of the position they shared. Now, that was gone. Edmund was now the heir and, as such, a step above a mere second son. His goals must now shift. His interest must change. His position was no longer one of equal rank. He was elevated both in title and in position as Richard's superior. They remained friends, of course, and always would, but it was not as it was. It was a fact which stung.

"You would be mistaken if you think he does not value your opinion."

Again he shrugged. "He may value my opinions, but that is all they are — theories devised through observation. What he needs is knowledge based on experience, and that I cannot give him."

She laid her hand on his arm, as thrilling a touch to her now as it had ever been. His arm was so firm beneath her fingers. She had always drawn comfort from his strength. He had always been ready to protect and defend her. It was his shoulder she had longed to weep on when her brother had been taken. It was his absence that had made her grieving so much more acute. "What he needs is the support of friends. That, you can give." There was no chiding in her voice, no pleading or coercing tone. It was stated as an unarguable fact.

Richard chuckled. "Always to the point, are you not, Harry? It is good to know some things remain the same." He placed his hand over hers. "Although, I may not have recognized you. You have become a beautiful young lady in the past two years. Do you have the young swains swooning at your feet? Is that why you have hidden away in the music room when you should be dancing the night away with the other debs?"

She coloured and lowered her eyes. "There are a few who gather, but none who interest."

"None good enough?" he teased, secretly glad no gentleman had yet captured her attention. "Is it their lack of standing, or do they have some hideous physical defect?"

She snatched her hand from him and stood, placing both hands on her hips. "Is this what you think of me? That I have changed so much in two years as to have no thought in my head that runs deeper than a gentleman's looks and the size of his bank account?"

"Do not fly into the bows, Harry. I was teasing. I know you have

LISTEN TO YOUR HEART

"Did you read the papers I sent you?" Anne de Bourgh questioned her cousin Fitzwilliam Darcy as soon as he entered the sitting room.

"I did." He nodded to Mrs. Jenkins. She smiled

and inclined her head in acceptance of his greeting before returning her focus to her stitching.

"And?" She looked at him expectantly, waiting for him to share his opinion of their content.

"You found them in your father's office?"

Anne nodded. "Between some books as if tucked away and out of sight intentionally."

"I had my solicitor look at them. They seem legitimate." He tipped his head to the side and gave her a questioning look. "They will change things for your mother. Are you sure you wish to take on that battle? Will your health tolerate it?"

"My health will never be robust, but I am not standing on the edge of the grave, Fitzwilliam." Anne laid aside her mending. "I intend to approach her today on one item."

"Today?" Darcy handed Anne a small glass of sherry and then picking up his own glass, settled into a comfortable chair near his cousin. "And what item is first on your list?"

Anne sipped her sherry and considered how she should approach the subject of their supposed engagement. "I have heard some troubling news. It seems my mother's imaginings regarding our future have travelled far and wide."

"She has never been one to keep that particular story to herself. I am surprised you had not realized the extent to which it is common knowledge. Makes it blasted hard to get to know any young ladies during the season — which, I suppose, is her intent in publishing the tale." His eyes narrowed, and his jaw clenched as he attempted to contain his frustration at his aunt's machinations.

"Yes, but at least you are free of these walls." Anne waved a hand around the room. "I have not even been given the opportunity to meet any eligible gentlemen, and I am nearly five and twenty! Firmly on the shelf having never left it! No longer. I will have it no longer."

Darcy's eyes grew wide in surprise.

"Today, my mother will know that her imaginings are just that — fanciful tales which hold no basis in reality. I am sorry, my dear cousin, but I do not now, nor have I ever, wished to marry you." She smiled at him. "I need not fear for my financial stability. Father has amply provided for me as those documents attest. I am at liberty to choose a match based on compatibility and, if I am so fortunate, love. And you might pursue such a match for yourself without scorn or derision from society as I am the one to call off this sham of an engagement."

Darcy sat slack-jawed, unable to know where to begin a reply to such a declaration, but Anne was not yet through.

"I believe I might be of assistance to you in finding ladies who would suit your temperament, but I will need you to place your trust in me." She placed her glass on the table and leaned toward Darcy. "I have studied your character for years, Fitzwilliam. I believe I am as qualified as you, if not more qualified, to find an acceptable match for you."

"You…" He shook his head to clear away the fog. "You will find a match for me?"

"Indeed I will, but first I must inform Mother of my decision to not marry you." Anne stood and walked to the window that looked out over the park toward the parsonage at Hunsford. "Mother has a new parson. Did you know?"

Darcy nodded. "Yes, I have met him. He was visiting relatives in Hertfordshire when I was there with Bingley."

"He was sent to find a wife from amongst his cousins." She watched Darcy's face discretely and bit back a smile at the horror that passed across his features. "He was successful in finding a wife...." She turned and paused purposefully. "They were married in January." The colour had drained completely from his face, and she wondered for a moment if she had gone too far in ascertaining the truth of Mrs. Collins' words regarding his feelings. They had shared many fascinating conversations regarding Darcy's stay in Hertfordshire. "It is unfortunate he did not choose to marry one of his cousins as such a marriage would have been to the family's advantage, what with the entail and all."

Darcy slumped forward and rested his head in his hands. "He did not marry a cousin?"

"No." Anne came to sit near him once more. "He married Miss Lucas. I assume you know of whom I speak. I have been given to understand her father is well-known in Hertfordshire." She studied how his shoulders relaxed and noticed him rub at the corner of one eye. She placed a hand on his shoulder and whispered. "The lady who is your heart's desire remains unattached." His body tensed under her touch, and she was certain his breathing had ceased. "Mrs Collins is her particular friend, it seems, and she, along with Mrs. Collin's sister, has come to stay at the parsonage for a visit. She has been here a fortnight, and I find I shall quite miss her when she leaves. So open and welcoming. Intelligent, too. It is through her I discovered just how much damage my mother's tales of our engagement might be causing." She withdrew her hand from his shoulder and sat back in her chair, waiting for his reaction.

"Elizabeth is here?" He whispered.

Anne smiled to herself. He was clearly more smitten than even Mrs Collins realized, and certainly more than Elizabeth would consider. "She is, and she is under the impression we are to marry should you ever be a gentleman and ask me."

THROUGH EVERY STORM

George Wickham slammed the glass down on the table. He had not meant to slam it down, but the table had somehow risen closer to his hand. He looked around the room, straining to find the barkeep. There appeared to be twice as many people here now as there had been mere minutes ago. Why could they not stay still instead of dancing in circles? He dropped his head into his hands.

"Come on, old boy, time to get you home."

Colonel Nathaniel Denny hoisted his friend up to a semi-standing position and placed an arm around the drunken man to steady him. This was not the first time he had come to cart Wickham home. No, at one time, this had been a regular routine. Out of how many scrapes had Denny steered this reckless rogue?

"I dunno wanna go hum," slurred Wickham. "I wanna go to the greeve."

"It is not your time to go to the grave, Wickham. Perhaps tomorrow, but for tonight you are going home." Denny dragged him out the door into the night. A cold, early spring rain was beginning to fall. Denny helped Wickham mount his horse before pulling the hat from his friend's head. Perhaps a cold shower would help sober him up. Wickham uttered a curse and grabbed at one of the hats floating in front of him. The jerking action nearly sent him sprawling onto the ground.

After manoeuvring his horse close to Wickham's, Denny helped right his friend once again. "Hold onto the saddle, old man. I will steer you home." Wickham grabbed the saddle and slumped forward. Confident that his friend would stay seated, Denny nudged his horse to walk. With one hand on his own reigns and one on Wickham's, he began the slow journey to Wickham's rented house.

Wickham shivered as the rain ran down his face and under the collar of his coat. The coldness of the rain and the night air brought back to him the pain he had been attempting to forget. "She's gone." He lifted his head long enough to spit out the words before slumping forward once again. The effort to stay upright was still too great.

"Yes, she is gone." Denny knew what few others knew. Wickham, though once a cad and a rake, had learned to love his wife—a wife who was forced upon him due to an ill-thought out plan for revenge. Theirs had been a hard life of scraping by, first on the meager earnings of an enlisted man and then, the poor profits from his shop.

In one respect, she had been good for him. His love for her had finally overcome his love of gambling and had helped him gain a desire to become a respectable gentleman. It was too bad that she had not returned his affection.

"You still have Thomas and Louisa. You must think of them now."

Wickham groaned. How was he to care for his

children on his own? Thomas he could mold into the man he never was, but Louisa — what did he know of helping a girl grow into womanhood? His experiences with women were the sort that he hoped his daughter would avoid. Kitty would help him. She was the only one of his wife's sisters who still spoke to him. The few bridges that he had not burned in his misguided youth, his wife had done a masterful job of destroying.

Denny pulled Wickham from his horse and helped him into the house. He poured some cold black coffee into a mug and shoved it at his friend. Wickham grimaced at the taste of the stale coffee.

"You could go after her." Denny took a seat across from Wickham.

"And do what? Get myself killed?" Wickham scoffed.

"That is what you are trying to do now. At least if death comes at the end of a dueling pistol instead of the bottom of a bottle, it would be an honourable death."

"Honourable." Wickham huffed. "When have I ever been honourable?" He took another gulp of his coffee and placed the cup on the table.

Denny pushed the mug toward him and raised

a brow in challenge. Wickham sighed and took possession of the drink again.

"In the past five years," said Denny, "you have proven yourself to be honourable on many occasions."

"Those were not honourable actions, but restitution. There is a difference."

"Only an honourable man would make payment for his past transgressions. You, ten years ago, would have scoffed at any man who tried to right his own or another person's wrongs–in fact, you did. How many times did I hear you curse the name of Darcy?"

Wickham stared at the dark liquid in his cup. "I should have listened to him–to him, his father and my own. Instead, I blamed them for all my misfortunes. Stupid man." Wickham gulped the last of his coffee. "Stupid, stupid man."

Denny slapped the table. "You are that man no longer. Pull yourself together, and get on with life." Denny had never had much patience for wallowing. It was what made him a good leader. He could be empathetic with his men, but he did not abide a sustained time of self-pity. He stood with his arms crossed, glowering down at Wickham. "Go to bed. We will plan your attack on life in the morning."

Wickham laughed. "I am not in the militia anymore, my friend."

"No. But you are in a battle nonetheless. Now, go to bed."

Wickham stood shakily and gave a limp and misaimed salute. Bed sounded like a welcome prospect. With any luck, perhaps he would wake from this nightmare in the morning.

~*~*~*~*~*~

Morning came, bright and clear — far too bright for Wickham. Denny threw open the curtains in Wickham's room and called loudly to his friend. "Get up. The day awaits."

Wickham groaned and rolled away from the light. "Have a care, Denny. My head feels like it has been trampled by a horse. Keep your voice down and the curtains drawn."

"I will do nothing of the sort. You shall feel the full extent of what you have done to yourself. Perhaps you will remember it the next time you wish to drown your sorrows." He yanked the pillow from under Wickham's head, causing his friend to curse as his head bounced off the mattress. "Dress and be down in ten. Do not test me." Denny threw a set of clothes at him and left the room, deliberately slamming the door.

Grumbling and sputtering, Wickham rushed to dress. He knew from experience that Denny made no idle threats.

"Why must I arise so early and is such haste?" Wickham demanded when he appeared below stairs.

"Sit and eat." Denny motioned to the plate of food on the table. "We need to travel."

Wickham took his seat at the table. "Travel? Where? And what of my children?"

"Your children are with my wife, where they will remain until I see that you are indeed ready to be their father again." He stared at Wickham through narrowed eyes until Wickham took up his utensils and began eating. " We're going to Derbyshire."

Wickham nearly choked on the bit of egg he had just popped into his mouth. "Why would I go to Derbyshire?"

"They are expecting us."

"How can they be expecting us?" Wickham had had no communication with Fitzwilliam Darcy in years, save to send bits of money in repayment of the money he had demanded of Darcy, money which had been an inducement to marry. He was quite certain that Pemberley was one place where he was not welcome.

About the Author

Leenie Brown has always been a girl with an active imagination, which, while growing up, was a both an asset, providing many hours of fun as she played out stories, and a liability, when her older sister and aunt would tell her frightening tales. At one time, they had her convinced Dracula lived in the trunk at the end of the bed she slept in when visiting her grandparents!

Although it has been years since she cowered in her bed in her grandparents' basement, she still has an imagination which occasionally runs away with her, and she feeds it now as she did then — by reading!

Her heroes, when growing up, were authors, and the worlds they painted with words were (and still are) her favourite playgrounds! She was that child, under the covers with the flashlight, reading until the wee hours of the morning...and pretending not to be tired the next day so her mother wouldn't find out.

In addition to feeding her imagination, she also exercises it — by writing. While writing has been an activity she has dabbled in over the years, it blossomed into a full-fledged obsession when she stumbled upon the world of Jane Austen Fan Fiction. Leenie had first fallen in love with Jane Austen's work in her early teens when she was captivated by the tale of a girl, who like her, was the second born of five daughters. Now, as an adult, she spends much time in the regency world, playing with the characters from her favourite Jane Austen novels and a few that are of her own creation.

When she is not traipsing down a trail in an attempt to keep up with her imagination, Leenie resides in the beautiful province of Nova Scotia with her two sons and her very own Mr. Brown (a wonderful mix of all the best of Darcy, Bingley and Edmund with a healthy dose of the teasing Mr. Tilney and just a dash of the scolding Mr. Knightley).

Connect with Leenie Brown

Want to know what Leenie is working on now or when the next book will be released?
Follow her on
Twitter:
@LeenieBAuthor
Facebook:
www.facebook.com/LeenieBrownAuthor
or her blog:
leeniebrown.com
She can also be found on
AustenAuthors.net
Or you can contact her by email at
LeenieBrownAuthor@gmail.com

You Might Also Enjoy...

FROM AUTHOR ROSE FAIRBANKS

UNDONE BUSINESS

November 26, 1811

Netherfield looked as opulent as any house from the ton, adorned in flowers from the conservatory. The couples around them laughed and conversed. Despite the general gaiety of the evening, Fitzwilliam Darcy and Elizabeth Bennet remained silent as they went down the dance. At long last, Mr. Darcy asked his partner, "Do you and your sisters often walk to Meryton?" They turned about each other.

"Yes, nearly daily." She paused and raised her

eyebrows. "When you met us there the other day, we had just been forming a new acquaintance."

Immediately, Darcy felt his body tense as he fought to keep his face from turning red in anger. He glared at Elizabeth. "Mr. Wickham is blessed with such happy manners as may ensure his making friends—whether he may be equally capable of retaining them, is less certain."

"He has been so unlucky as to lose your friendship," replied Elizabeth, "and in a manner which he is likely to suffer from all his life."

His irritation redoubled as he realised Wickham had actually found opportunity sometime in the last rain-soaked week to speak to her. Darcy imagined Wickham sitting beside her, inhaling her tantalizing rosewater scent, and smiling charmingly while putting her at ease. His lies of woe likely played on Elizabeth's tender heart, but Darcy could say or do nothing without possibly exposing his sister. He tried to change the subject.

"What think you of books?"

Elizabeth refused to consider the topic and instead returned to Wickham. "You are careful in the creation of your implacable resentment, are you not?"

"I am," he said in a firm voice. How could she believe Wickham?

"And never allow yourself to be blinded by prejudice?"

"I hope not."

"It is particularly incumbent on those who never change their opinion, to be secure of judging properly at first."

"May I ask to what these questions tend?"

"Merely to the illustration of your character. I am trying to make it out."

"And what is your success?"

She shook her head. "I do not get on at all. I hear such different accounts of you as puzzle me exceedingly."

"I can readily believe," answered he gravely, "that reports may vary greatly with respect to me, and I could wish, Miss Bennet, that you were not to sketch my character at the present moment, as there is reason to fear that the performance would reflect no credit on either."

"But if I do not take your likeness now, I may never have another opportunity."

"I would by no means suspend any pleasure of yours," he coldly replied.

She said no more, and they went down the other dance and parted in silence. He wished to be angry at Elizabeth but found all of it centred on Wickham. How had he targeted her? She was the one person who could tempt him to explain his history with Wickham. He resolved to find a way to warn her without exposing Georgiana. He hoped, rather than believed, he only desired to protect her instead of improve her opinion of him.

From Author April Floyd

THE PARSON OF PEMBERLEY

Chapter One

Mary Bennet gazed through the rainy window of the parlor listening to her crowd of sisters speaking of balls, soldiers and Netherfield Park. To her peaceful mind it all amounted to so much jangling noise. She preferred her Bible, reflecting upon the word was her reward for enduring the company of her younger sisters.

The sisters Bennet were forever disdainful of her presence and so never noticed her ability to be a chameleon in their presence. She knew of Lydia's plans for any man in uniform who might glance her way. She knew Kitty would expect perhaps more in a man than Lydia. She knew Jane would be the beauty to land Charles Bingley and Elizabeth the one likely to drive any suitor to madness.

Mary longed for a man of faith. One who might be satisfied with an evening before the fire discussing the apostle Paul or the Beatitudes or perhaps with her playing the pianoforte while he prepared a sermon for his flock.

She startled from her reverie at the queries of her younger sisters regarding a ball at Netherfield. "Mary, undoubtedly, a ball is not an event you aspire to attend?" Kitty asked in a manner that left Mary resentful of having to answer with her entire family gathered.

"The dance in Meryton was quite satisfactory. I have no desire to attend a ball at Netherfield, should there ever be one, thank you kindly." Mary replied to Kitty without giving her further attention.

"Lizzie, do you think the snobbish Mr. Darcy would attend a ball at Netherfield? For all that Mr.

Bingley is his dearest friend, he does not seem well suited to their friendship." Lydia wondered aloud.

"Lydia Bennet! It is neither my particular concern nor desire to be subjected to Mr. Darcy and his dour manner. If he decides to attend a ball at Netherfield, I should be certain it was for Caroline Bingley's benefit." Lizzie sighed, peevish at the subject of Mr. Darcy.

"Mr. Bennet do you see? Lizzie might put forth an effort to catch Mr. Darcy's eye, haughty and rude though he may be, and she has already cast him aside as unsuitable!" Mrs. Bennet fretted twisting her handkerchief. "Thank heaven for our sweet Jane! She has the beauty and the good sense to set her sights for Mr. Bingley."

"Yes, dear. I do see. Our girls should never allow a man the fair advantage. They must always be as hounds to the fox."

Jane smiled at Lizzie as their father teased their mother. "Lizzie, dear, I find Mr. Darcy to be a quiet man, not given to frivolous chatter and shallow sentiment." Jane spoke so that only Lizzie might hear; she did not wish the family to discuss her sister's dilemma. Jane knew that Lizzie was drawn to the mysterious man but the pride she held dear would prevent her from admitting her attraction, especially after his snub in Meryton regarding her appearance.

Mary excused herself, not that her sisters noticed. She took her Bible upstairs to her small room and sat upon her bed. Her head ached from the schemes and machinations of her mother regarding the marriages of her daughters. Whatever became of love and mutual regard?

Mary had yet to contrive for a man and certainly none had taken notice. Her sisters stood out as colorful birds alongside her quiet, dignified presence. Shortly, she heard their footsteps, giggles, and whispers as they came upstairs to change for dinner.

Mama was convinced her favorite child would win Mr. Bingley's favor and save the family from the certain doom of the entailment which shadowed Mrs. Bennet's every waking moment. Papa was more thoughtful of late since receiving letters last week, one in particular. Mary wondered at Mr. Bennet's distraction.

Elizabeth and Jane held their secrets, though Mary was more mature than Kitty or Lydia. While accustomed to the slight, it remained on her heart.

Being the quiet, oft- ignored sister provided her with an unlikely opportunity to hear the whispered words and quiet exchanges of her elder sisters.

It was thus she decided the Good Book was her only refuge, a solace when those around her passed her over or dismissed her words. She knew there must be at least one man in all of England who harbored the same feelings as she.

Regardless, she took her meals upstairs for a time to avoid the stir their new neighbors invoked upon Longbourn.

Chapter Two

Mary descended the stairs of an afternoon to find her mother in the sway of one of her customary attacks. An invitation had arrived for Jane from Miss Bingley. Mama had one of the maids return an answer to Netherfield as quickly as she might, even with the sky the color of her slate upstairs.

"Do you think it wise to accept a dinner invitation with uncertain weather approaching?" Mary asked and glanced to Jane as she moved to sit beside her in the parlor. Mrs. Bennet waved her arms and hushed Mary. "Please do be quiet! If the rains delay until Jane is well and truly inside Netherfield then perhaps she may enjoy a private moment with Mr. Bingley!" Jane patted Mary's hand, all the while noticing the flecting expression of hurt that crossed her face like the shadow of a cloud against the sun.

"Jane, my dear, you must take a horse and not the carriage. We've not one to spare, you see. And should indeed rains descend upon us, you will remain at Netherfield until the weather has cleared! Yes, what a splendid plan!" Mrs. Bennet was pleased with herself at the circumstance she plotted. Jane was a bit more unsettled, wishing not to seem conniving as her mother.

"Upstairs with you!" Mrs. Bennet instructed her eldest daughter as she turned to Mary still sitting upon the sofa. "Don't sit there bewildered Mary! Go have Hill send hot water for Jane's bath!"

Mary slowly rose from her seat and went in search of Hill, cross over her mother's disregard. She stood gazing from the back door as Hill instructed the kitchen maids regarding the hot water for Miss Jane. Mary watched as two young maids struggled at the back stairs with their burden. She turned to the door and saw her younger sisters making their way home, laughing and dealing nonsense, no doubt.

She made her way to her room and sat down at the pianoforte. Her practice would set her family on edge but the exercise comforted her. Besides, she was in no mood to either see Jane off or listen to the foolish chatter of Lydia and Kitty as they gave detail of the soldiers in Meryton.

Lizzie knocked on her door several times before she relented and walked away. Mary heard Jane in the hallway and her sister's cries at how lovely she appeared. Lizzie made her usual fuss over Jane's hair and Mrs. Bennet called for Lydia and Kitty to allow her room to breathe.

Mary peeped from her door once the commotion in the hall ceased. She tiptoed to the bannister so that she might see them without participating in their conversation or the flutter about Jane.

Jane was quite lovely, her face aglow with first love. Her dress was an exact shade of sky blue and her cloak and bonnet made a striking compliment in a darker hue of the same color. The horse was saddled and brought round front as the skies darkened. Jane was apprehensive at first, uneasy at the coming storm, but the will of Mrs. Bennet would not be subdued.

Lizzie followed her sister and family outdoors, worry creasing her forehead as she glanced to the clouds. She smiled for Jane though, and reassured her as she smoothed her skirts and cloak as she sat upon the horse. "Oh Lizzie, I wish you were coming along!" Jane called as the horse moved down the lane. Elizabeth sighed and kept watch until Jane disappeared.

The Bennet ladies retreated to the parlor. "Hill, we will be ready for dinner soon. Please let Mr. Bennet know that Jane has gone." Mrs. Bennet sniffed, irritated that her husband hadn't left his library for Jane's departure.

"Mary, you should come into Meryton with us on the morrow." Lydia giggled. "There are so many men. I am sure one might be interested in a quiet lady without a penchant for fun." Kitty snorted laughter as she taunted Mary.

Lizzie hushed them both. "Mary isn't the foolish one running about town causing tongues to wag regarding her behavior. Mama, you might be more concerned about your youngest daughters now that Jane is likely to capture Mr. Bingley's heart. "

Mrs. Bennet fixed Elizabeth with a sneer. "At least they are capable of drawing the interest of a suitor, unlike yourself or Mary. Mr. Bennet and I cannot keep you into your years Elizabeth, nor Mary." She pointed her folded fan imperiously towards Elizabeth during this set down.

Mary dismissed herself from their company and was followed by her younger sisters. On the stairs they tried apologizing but Mary wasn't listening. Her mother's words played over in her head. She mumbled something to Lydia and Kitty, leaving them to enter her room and close the door. She lay upon the bed, tears flowing freely that none would witness.

From Author Zoe Burton

PROMISES KEPT

As Elizabeth sat in the slow-moving carriage, looking out the window at the hustle and bustle of London, her mind was elsewhere. She was thinking back to the ride she shared with her husband yesterday.

He had ordered their horses saddled before leaving his dressing room. After rousing her from sleep, he persuaded her to go with him. After breaking their fast, they rode to the outskirts of the city, to a large empty field. To her surprise, there was a track worn into the grass all around the edge. She was further surprised to be challenged by her husband to a race. Never one to let such a provocation go unanswered, she agreed. Around and around the field they raced, for seven laps. The groom who had accompanied them was pressed into service to count the laps and to wave a handkerchief to signal the end of the contest.

Lizzy was thrilled with the feeling of the horse moving under her, the thudding of his hooves hitting the ground vibrating up through her bottom, and the air whizzing past her face. Clucking her tongue and tapping him with her riding crop, she urged the horse to go faster and faster, first to catch up to Fitzwilliam, and then to pass him. They ran neck and neck for a while, and at the end she beat him by just a nose. Exhilarated, she cheered, shrieking her joy in a most unladylike fashion, raising her arms high in the air, then bringing them down to clap loudly. Her husband laughed out loud. Her joy was infectious and he enjoyed seeing it. This was his goal in bringing his beloved wife to this place. He knew that she loved racing her friends and family. She had not had opportunity in a long while to do so.

Bringing her horse around, she trotted him up close beside her husband's. Giving Fitzwilliam a cheeky smile, she leaned over for kiss.

"Very good, Sweetheart. I did not know you were capable of such a feat," he said to her with a laugh.

"Did you not?" she asked, teasing him in return. "I certainly did. Both my horse and I are so much younger than you; 'twas not a difficult task." She tossed her head as she spoke, raising her nose in the air as she had seen so many high society women do in recent days during her visits. Her words and manner drew another laugh from Fitzwilliam. Drawing his horse to a stop and dismounting, he reached for her, pulling her out of the saddle and into his arms. As the groom, with eyes averted, led the horses away for a further cool-down, Elizabeth's joyous laugh was suddenly stopped by her husband's ardent kiss.

Elizabeth's companions in the carriage, her Aunt Gardiner and Lady Matlock, looked at her smile then at each other. It was obvious that their niece was present only physically. Mentally she was somewhere else entirely.

Cocking her eyebrow and nodding to Elizabeth, the Lady silently asked a question. With a shrug, Madelyn Gardiner tipped her head in acquiescence. Clearing her throat, she directed a question to Elizabeth.

"Lizzy?"

No response. She tried again, this time a little louder.

"Lizzy?"

Nothing. Seeing Lady Matlock covering a smile with her hand, Mrs. Gardiner rolled her eyes before trying another time a little more loudly, this time adding in a quick nudge with her elbow.

"Elizabeth!"

Elizabeth jumped, startled out of her daydream. Her hand to her chest, she cried, "What?" After having jumped a bit themselves, her aunts sputtered before dissolving into laughter. Soon they had laughed so hard, tears were running down their faces.

The object of their amusement was rather offended at first. They were laughing at her, and she did not know why. However, her natural tendency toward humour and the infectiousness of their merriment soon overtook her, and she joined in.

As they began to calm, Mrs. Gardiner inquired, "What were you thinking about, Lizzy? I called and called to you, and you never heard me."

Elizabeth smiled as a blush stole over her cheeks. "I was thinking about the race Fitzwilliam and I had yesterday."

"Race? What kind of race?"

"After we broke our fast, he invited me for a ride out to the edge of town. There is a nice large field there, about an acre and a half in size, I believe he said. There is a track worn around the outside of it, and he dared me to race him. You know, Aunt Maddie, how I respond to challenges."

Mrs. Gardiner laughed, "Oh, yes, I do! Please, I am all curiosity now; continue."

With a smile, Elizabeth did so. "There is not much left to tell. We completed several laps, and our groom started us, kept track of the circuits we made, then waved a handkerchief to indicate the end. It was so very enjoyable! I loved the feel of the wind and the pounding of the hooves of my horse vibrating up through the saddle. I have not felt so free, nor so...self-assured in a long time!" She leaned forward, an eager smile on her face, her eyes brighter than they had seen in weeks, and it was clear to her listeners how enthralled she was with the experience.

Lady Matlock was worried. "But, Elizabeth, it is so dangerous! A lady's stirrup has no hold for your foot! You could have fallen and been injured or killed!"

"Oh, no, Aunt Audra; Fitzwilliam had my stirrups switched to the regular iron ones like his. He said that sidesaddles are dangerous enough, and he does not want to be constantly worrying about me when I'm riding. I know it's not terribly fashionable yet, but I have seen other ladies using them. Please do not worry."

"Very well, then. I know that Fitzwilliam is deliberate in everything he does. I will trust his judgment in this." Lady Matlock turned teasing, asking, "Just who won this contest?"